DEADWOOD
Shorts

Fa~~mily~~ tal
Traditions

Ann Charles

Illustrated by C.S. Kunkle

Dear Reader,

When I sat down to start plotting the 11th book in the Deadwood Mystery Series, I realized that something was missing in the series—a transitional story in the overall series needing to be told in order to wrap up the previous ten novels and prepare you for the next many books to come. At that point, FATAL TRADITIONS was born.

New Year's Eve seemed like the perfect time to set this story. For so many of us, the end of the year is when we tend to look back at what joys and obstacles we've experienced in the past and make big plans for our future. Violet agreed with my way of thinking, the only stipulation being that tequila was somehow involved. If she was going to explore her family's long and blood-filled history, she needed something to make it easier to swallow what she feared filled the pages of the leather-bound book Aunt Zoe had been asking her to read for months.

If you have read the 5th book in my Jackrabbit Junction Series, you know that Natalie, Cooper, and Ol' Man Harvey are in Arizona over the New Year's holiday trying to enjoy some sunshine while they work out some kinks. (If you haven't read IN CAHOOTS WITH THE PRICKLY PEAR POSSE and are a fan of Cooper and Natalie and Harvey, you might want to read that story for some Arizona-inspired "heat" and chuckles.) With these three out of state, Violet and the rest of her crew are left to bring in the New Year with plenty of hilarity and chills.

I hope you enjoy this extra-long Deadwood Short about the past and future for our favorite *Scharfrichter*. Grab a drink for the "read" and toast with Violet and me to past blunders and future laughs as we roll along the pages into a new Deadwood year.

www.anncharles.com

Praise for Ann Charles'

Fatally Traditions

"I want to spend next New Year's Eve with Violet and her crew in Deadwood!" ~**T.S. Owen**

"A creep level that whets the appetite for gore and all the things that make ya go hhhhmm." ~**Mary Avery**

"Spend your New Year's Eve with Violet and her gang for a party that you will not forget." ~**Laura Wollam**

"Ringing out the old year with some spooky fun and a whole lot of hair raising family history as Violet plots how to survive the new year." ~**J.W. Reinhold**

"Tequila, food, games and family ring in the New Year talking monsters and the women who take them down." ~**Heather Chargualaf**

"Mix New Year's with family game night and some great characters for a party we won't forget!" ~**Vicki Huskey**

"Come catch the chills in Boo-ville, a boarded up town with ghouls and ghosts around every corner and the only cure is the friends surrounding you." ~**Craig Watts Scott**

"New Year's Eve Party Time:
Family game night √
Tequila √
Delicious treats √
Spooky stories sure to fuel your nightmares √
What more could you ask for?" ~**Rebecca Lyndsey**

"A New Year's Eve slumber party full of lovable characters, yummy goodies and a gory family history that will leave you craving more." ~**Michelle Davis**

"Violet Parker, the reluctant *Scharfrichter*, learns more than she cares to about the fates of the long line of executioners of the past." ~**Rob Grayson**

"Violet Parker is ringing in the New Year with stories of her *Scharfrichter* ancestors throbbing in her head. Can she live up to the legacy of her family's tradition in the upcoming year?" ~**Diane Garland, Your WorldKeeper**

For more information about Ann and her books, check out her website, as well as the reader reviews for her books on Amazon, Barnes & Noble, and Goodreads.

Deadwood Shorts: Fatal Traditions

Copyright © 2019 by Ann Charles

All rights reserved. Except as permitted under the U.S. Copyright Act of 1976, no part of this publication may be reproduced, distributed, or transmitted in any form or by any means now known or hereafter invented, or stored in a database or retrieval system, without the prior written permission of the author, Ann Charles.

This book is a work of fiction. Names, characters, places, and incidents are the product of the author's imagination or are used fictitiously. Any resemblance to actual persons, living or dead, business establishments, events, or locales is coincidental.

Cover Design by Boe Biddles
Edited by Eilis Flynn (www.emsflynn.com)

Library of Congress - 2019915176
E-book ISBN- 978-1-940364-67-4
Print ISBN-:13: 978-1-940364-68-1

Also by Ann Charles

To Mark and Michelle Davis

You are amazingly generous and loads of fun!

Thank you for stepping forward and offering to help when my promotional tank was running low on creativity.

You make this journey through the pages even more wonderful.

Acknowledgments

While I have a tendency to wax on eloquently (and sometimes not) according to one particular long-time writing buddy of mine (*cough … Jacquie Rogers … cough*), short stories mean I keep the acknowledgments short, too.

Thank you to my husband, kids, family, friends, graphic artist, artist, editors, first-draft readers, local expert, world keeper, beta readers, promotion team, and four keyboard-sitting cats. Thanks also to my brother, Clint, for exploring Deadwood's Chinese Tunnels with me when we were kids.

Special thanks to my good author friend, Kristy McCaffrey, for giving me a great cover quote and for cheering me on chapter after chapter.

Also, a big THANK YOU to Black Hills Paranormal Investigations (Maurice "Mo" Miller, Mark Shadley, Deb Sutton, LeAnn Harlan, Dani-Jo Butler, Kayleigh Johnson) for helping me pick out the "tools" to hunt ghosts in Boo-ville.

Thank you to all who keep me in the writing business, support my addiction to telling stories, and enjoy spending time with me and the side effects of my warped brain on the page. Without you, I would still be sneaking steamy sex scenes and gruesome murder tales into the technical documents at a banking software company.

Cast

Violet Lynn Parker—Heroine of the series, real estate agent

Dane "Doc" Nyce—Violet's boyfriend, medium

Zoe Parker—Violet's aunt and mentor in life

Layne Parker—Violet's nine-year-old son

Cornelius Curion—Violet's client; so-called ghost-whisperer

Reid Martin—Captain of the fire dept., Aunt Zoe's ex-lover

"Courage is being scared to death and saddling up anyway."

~John Wayne

Chapter One

As badass killers went, most days I couldn't drive a nail into a coffin with a sledgehammer. So how in the hell did I have a chance at catching a Hungarian devil that morphed into black smoke every time I came within grabbing distance, let alone executing it if shit went south?

"Violet," Aunt Zoe said as she joined me in the kitchen. In her yellow and red paisley silk loungewear and silver-streaked hair pulled back in a ponytail, she looked a decade younger than her fifty-plus years. "Do we have any ..." She paused when she looked over at me, her brow wrinkling. "What'd you do to your hair?"

I glanced down at my blond ends that were normally a crazy curly mess. "I straightened it."

She moved closer, taking a strand in her fingers. She smelled like the molasses cookies she'd baked earlier for tonight's New Year's Eve fun and games. "Doesn't that damage your hair?"

"If I did it all of the time, sure."

She stepped back, one dark eyebrow inching up.

"What's the special occasion?"

I shrugged. "Maybe it's time for a change."

Her blue eyes narrowed. "What's spurring this change?"

"I've been thinking about a few things is all." I tried to play it cool, hiding behind a double-wide smile as if I hadn't been chewing my knuckles about that damned Hungarian devil all afternoon.

"Baby girl, I can see clear through that glass smile." Unfortunately, Aunt Zoe wasn't easy to hornswoggle. I'd have better luck pushing a wet noodle through a keyhole.

I sidestepped her and made a beeline for the bottles of tequila and whiskey sitting on top of the refrigerator. A change of subject was in order. "I've been thinking about our family history book."

The "book" was more of a tell-all tome about my female ancestors, only instead of sharing my great-great-grandmother's favorite recipes, it told about those who had slain before me and *what* had perished due to their deft hands. It also shared which ancestors hadn't been so successful along with how they'd come to their end.

Much to my chagrin, because each of us "exterminators" were unique like freaking snowflakes, these anecdotes only gave ideas on what *might* work in the heat of a kill-or-be-killed moment. In my trade as an Executioner—or *Scharfrichter* as they liked to call us in the Black Forest region of Germany where my ancestors first ran roughshod over troublemakers—there were no sure methods to the madness of ridding the world of the vermin that preyed on the innocent.

But enough whining about circumstances that were beyond my fingertips these days.

Aunt Zoe crossed her arms. "What about the book?"

"Does Doc still have it?" I set the bottles on the counter next to the basket of lemons and limes, making brief eye contact.

My boyfriend, Doc Nyce, liked reading historical books almost as much as he liked playing doctor with me. He had volunteered to read my ancestors' book for me since I had an aversion to non-fiction literature that made me want to hide under my bed from monsters 24/7.

Doc claimed he aspired to help me become a better killer, but I had a suspicion he also wanted to understand who was sharing a bed with him most nights and take precautions on how *not* to end up dead himself. I had a history of wicked nightmares. If I were to wake up swinging, Doc needed to be ready to bob and weave.

Aunt Zoe watched me with a squint that would have made an Old West gunslinger tip his hat. "I have the book right now. I've been adding to it. Why?"

What was she adding?

Aunt Zoe was my designated career biographer, sharing my professional résumé for those killers who were next in line after me. Whatever she was writing on the pages was probably about my track record as an Executioner so far. Was she writing about the clusterfuck in Slagton earlier this month? Or my last run-in with the bone cruncher? Or one of my other fumbling attempts at catching fiends?

"I'd like to take a look at it again," I told her.

"Again?" she scoffed. "You didn't read it the last time I gave it to you."

"I scanned it." Sort of. The first few pages anyway.

"You fell asleep reading it and then you lost it."

"I didn't lose it, Layne took it without telling me."

My nearly ten-year-old son was also a bookhound. While he wasn't Doc's kid biologically, Layne followed in Doc's footsteps in both a fascination with the past along with the weapons used to keep the peace—or destroy it. Unlike Doc, though, my son didn't know that the book was about my female ancestors, or that his mother was most recent in line to take up the executioner's hood. He just pilfered interesting-looking books from his mom while she was getting her beauty rest.

"What exactly are you looking for in the book?" Aunt Zoe asked.

"Uhhh … something."

"Violet Lynn," she warned, her teeth sinking into my hide.

Hobknocker! Aunt Zoe was my *magistra*, which she explained meant she was responsible for teaching me as much as possible about how to be the best Executioner I could be. As a bonus, she also wanted to keep me from ending up like so many names in my family tree— prematurely dead—which would be great because it turned out I was extremely allergic to dying young.

"Okay, okay," I said, giving in to *that* look from her. "I'm searching for some ideas."

"Ideas for what?"

"Ideas on how to catch a Hungarian devil." I went back to the fridge for the bottles of root beer and lemon-lime soda pop, setting them on the counter next to the others.

"The *lidérc*," she said with a scowl, using its proper name. "I wish you'd reconsider this task."

"I can't and you know it."

I'd made a deal with the devil … well, not the Hungarian one, rather another more charming one, only he didn't turn to smoke when I got too close. Instead, Dominick Masterson tried to beguile me into doing his will, as in evil deeds and more. Luckily, the only reaction the slick prick triggered in me was extreme nausea.

Aunt Zoe wasn't so fortunate, though, both when it came to resisting Dominick's spell and staying off his radar. Even worse, the tricky bastard was obsessed with her, and no amount of self-protection she used to keep him at bay worked. That was where my deal with the handsome devil came into play. I'd catch one *lidérc* for him in exchange for

Aunt Zoe's permanent freedom from his sticky clutches.

"Maybe there's some other way," she said, but her tone had a weary note in it.

"There is no other way and you know it."

Aunt Zoe grabbed several glasses from the cupboard. "There aren't any accounts in the book of our predecessors successfully catching a *lidérc*."

"Yeah, but maybe—"

"Let alone eliminating one for good."

I cursed under my breath. "But there were tales of Executioners who fought and lost, right?"

"A few." The glasses clinked on the counter. She turned to me, her expression pinched. "It seems there was a point in the late Middle Ages when one particular *lidérc* took out two of our ancestors in a row within a year's time—they were identical twins."

Twins were also entwined in our ancestral thread, along with killers. I had a pair of fraternal ones myself. Twins, that was, not killers.

Addy, Layne's minutes-older sister, was spending the night with her best friend. Unfortunately, she hadn't taken her pet chicken, Elvis, with her, leaving me to babysit the busybody bird who liked to molt on my comforter and lay eggs in my shoes. Motherhood was full of surprises for me—first twins and then a dang chicken.

"Luckily," Aunt Zoe continued, "there were others in our line left to take up the fight after they both perished."

From the little I'd learned hands-almost-on about Hungarian devils, it appeared they had a leg up on Executioners by being non-human. However, that didn't mean they weren't mortal. Just more slippery than a pocket full of tapioca pudding, which meant I'd need to be extra wary.

"Maybe if we study their failures," I thought aloud, "we can figure out what *not* to do."

Aunt Zoe shook her head.

"Come on," I said. "You didn't even swish that notion around in your mouth before spitting it out."

"Violet, I don't like you going anywhere near the *lidérc*. Period."

"What then?"

"Let me go," she said. "Dominick is attractive. I could fare much worse."

"Bzzzt. Wrong answer." There was no way in hell I was letting that bastard win my favorite aunt. Besides, I needed her to help me navigate these Executioner waters.

She sighed, squeezing the bridge of her nose.

"I have to capture the *lidérc* ... or kill Dominick." Neither would be easy and both could result in a nasty ending—mine as well as theirs.

"Violet," she started.

I held up a hand for her to stop right there. "You know I'm right." Even if this was one of the few times I didn't want to be right, damn it.

Her chin jutted. "I know no such thing."

"And," I continued with my own matching chin jut, "if anything were to happen to me, you would still be around to protect and help Addy."

Our killer lineage was already rearing its head in my daughter. It was evident in the way she skillfully hefted bats and swung swords and other makeshift weapons, as well as by the sixth-sense ability that showed up in her dreams. While I'd rather this gene skipped over her, I smiled with pride at the "girl power" already rising within her. Lord help the teenage boy who broke her heart.

The doorbell rang.

Aunt Zoe and I both looked toward the dining room.

"That's probably Doc," I lied, knowing very well who I'd invited to our private little New Year's Eve party: Reid Martin, Deadwood's very own fire captain and Aunt Zoe's ex-heartthrob.

I'd run into Reid yesterday morning while grabbing some lattes at the Tin Cup Café. He'd looked extra handsome in his black flannel shirt and cowboy hat, reminding me of Sam Elliott when he acted in that Louis L'Amour movie with Tom Selleck—which one was it? Oh yeah, *The Sacketts*.

Anyway, when he'd asked if Doc and I had any fun plans for the holiday, I'd caved and invited him to join us.

All right, so maybe *caved* should be more like *jumped up and down with excitement*. I couldn't help it. I had big Cupid-inspired daydreams about seeing my aunt and him rekindle their old flame. Was it so wrong to dump a little gasoline on the bonfire when she wasn't looking?

Reid's eyes had lit up at my invitation, his smile spreading a mile wide under his mustache when I mentioned that not only was Aunt Zoe going to be there, but it was actually a slumber party and my son had insisted on a dress code for all attendees—sleepwear only.

"Doc?" Aunt Zoe's laser glare sizzled me from head to toe. Godzilla had nothing on her. Wait. Godzilla shot an atomic heat beam out of his mouth, not eyes. Never mind.

"Why would Doc ring the doorbell, Violet?"

Crap. That was a good question.

Doc had been spending most nights here with me lately, living out of a duffle bag. What had started with me nursing him through some bruised ribs had turned into a continual need for a nightly "nurse" that I didn't want to end.

Although, being that he had his own house a few blocks away, I couldn't expect him to stay forever. Working in my favor were the two other "roomies" sharing his now-crowded bachelor pad; however, Detective Cooper and his uncle, Harvey, were currently down in Arizona enjoying the sunshine with Natalie, who'd been my best friend since I stopped shoving peas and raisins up my nose for fun.

I fully expected Doc to want to stay in his own bed for a few nights while his roommates were gone to enjoy some alone time. After all, Aunt Zoe's place was at full-house capacity, and sharing two bathrooms wasn't always pleasant, especially when the one closest to my bedroom often had pink toothpaste globs stuck on the sink basin and fingerprint smudges all over the mirror.

"Uhhh, Doc would ring the doorbell because …" I tried not to grimace in anticipation of what Aunt Zoe was going to do to me when she found Reid standing on her front porch. "Maybe he lost his key."

She huffed. "The door isn't locked."

The doorbell rang again.

I struggled not to wince.

Footfalls pounded down the stairs. "Isn't anyone going to get that?" Layne called out.

I gulped. "Maybe Doc's hands are full of stuff. He was going to stop at home and grab some food for our little party, remember?"

"Judging by the way your nose is twitching, I think *you* are full of stuff."

I covered my lie-telling appendage with my hand. "I don't know what you're talking about."

She cocked her head to the side, listening as the front door creaked open and Layne greeted our guest with a "Hey! I didn't know you were coming tonight." The door banged shut. "Mom and Aunt Zoe are in the kitchen."

"Violet." Aunt Zoe's whisper had a noose-ish threat underlying it. Good thing lynching bees had gone out of style in Deadwood. "If you invited Reid to come tonight, I'm going to—"

The floorboards creaked in the dining room.

I ducked and covered.

Chapter Two

L ayne raced into the kitchen carrying a box—a board game, judging by the shape of it. A drawing of a sheeted ghost with cut-out eyes covered half of the box lid.

Where in the heck had he gotten that?

"Mom! Mr. Curion brought this cool game for us to play." He set the game on the table and raced out of the room.

Cornelius?

Before I had a chance to breathe a sigh of relief that Aunt Zoe wouldn't be strapping me to the rack just yet, Cornelius Curion waltzed into the kitchen wearing the calf-length maroon robe I'd given him for Christmas. Below the hem, a pair of black lounge pants dotted with four-leaf clovers ended at socks decorated with big purple horseshoes arching over the toes.

Holy lucky charms!

My gaze bobbed back to the top of the tall Technicolored talisman. His usual stovepipe hat was missing. In its place was one of those furry Cossack hats like the one worn by Omar Sharif in *Dr. Zhivago*, only Cornelius's was black instead of gray, blending with his hair.

"Hello, Violet's aunt," he said to Aunt Zoe, bowing slightly in her direction.

"Hello, Violet's friend," she replied, her eyes sparkling. "I like your hat. It's quite furry."

"Thank you. I won it years ago at a haunted Russian castle in a game of rock-paper-scissors with a dead tsar."

"You're kidding." Aunt Zoe played along, pretending to gape in astonishment. "Was it the ghost of Ivan the Terrible?"

"No. It was Boris the Tedious. It seems he was so genuinely uninteresting that he bored himself to death by accident one cold winter day."

Aunt Zoe laughed. "Ah, it's wonderful to see you again, Cornelius. You're more fun than chasing chickens."

I sneered at her reference to my earlier race throughout the house trying to corral Addy's dang chicken into the basement for the night.

"Cornelius, what are you doing here?" I asked, perplexed by his appearance in my aunt's kitchen. The last I'd heard he was heading out of the country for a couple of weeks to visit his sister.

He stared back at me, his crinkled brow matching mine as he stroked his goatee. "Who are you?"

I planted my hands on my hips. He and I had played this who's-who game on the phone more times than Elvis and I both had toes. "Don't start that again."

Over the last few months, I'd learned the hard way that Cornelius liked to play with people—both the breathing and non-breathing sorts. Part paranormal investigator, part ghost pied piper, he had enough money passed down from his ancestors' big bank accounts to own the moniker of "eccentric weirdo" without giving a rat's ass what the rest of the world thought about him.

"You resemble someone I've met before." Cornelius closed the distance between us. "But your aura is darker and terribly swirly. Is this real?" He took a lock of my hair and tugged on it. Hard.

"Ouch!" I pulled free.

He reached for another strand of hair.

I caught his bony wrist, glaring at him. "Touch it again and I'll bite your fingers clean off."

"You certainly growl and snarl like Violet." He turned to Aunt Zoe. "Maybe someone should take her rectal temperature to make sure she's human?"

My aunt grinned. "I think we should leave the rubber glove treatment for Detective Cooper when he returns from Arizona."

I cringed. Although anal probing would be preferable to sitting across the interrogation table from the Deadwood detective most days. Preferable to hunting down a Hungarian devil, too. Maybe Cornelius had some distant relative who knew some voodoo spell that would help me in my hunt.

I wrinkled my nose at Cornelius. "Quit being a knucklehead. I straightened my hair for tonight."

He inspected my hairstyle, clearly not impressed. "Prove that you're not an evil doppelganger who's abducted the real Violet."

"How's this?" I pinched his forearm through his robe.

Cornelius yipped and took a step back. Rubbing his arm, he frowned down at my pajama shirt, which had the Heat Miser's chubby cheeks, red nose, and flaming hair front and center. The shirt was a gift from my kids years ago after my mother had told them that *The Year Without a Santa Claus* was one of my childhood favorites.

His gaze shifted lower. "I'd wager that you fall under the fire sign."

"If this is a dig about my flaming pajama pants," I started.

"He's referring to astrology," Aunt Zoe explained. "And the four elements—air, water, earth, and fire."

Of course he was. Cornelius loved to talk about auras, chakras, and other new-age spirituality, hoochie-koo vibes.

"What are some of the fire sign traits?" I asked him.

"Passionate and temperamental."

"Don't forget quick to anger and physically strong," Aunt Zoe joined in, chuckling when I threatened her with my fist.

"Pow! Right in the kisser," I joked, in my best Jackie Gleason impression of Ralph Kramden from *The Honeymooners*.

"Bang! Zoom! You're going to the moon," Aunt Zoe shot back, tossing out more legendary lines from the old show.

"Aggressive and moody, too." Cornelius continued with his laundry list of my traits, which sounded more like faults. "She must be an Aries," he said to Aunt Zoe.

"Spot on, Cornelius," she said and clapped.

I rolled my eyes at his lucky guess. "I don't have time for a psych evaluation tonight."

"Impatient as well, like most Aries," Aunt Zoe said, still chuckling. "Cornelius has you nailed, baby girl."

"I'm going to nail him back—right to the basement wall, if he isn't careful. He can bring in the New Year with Elvis."

Cornelius slipped off his robe and draped it over a chair, nearly blinding me with his neon green pajama T-shirt. "Are you referring to the cultural rock-and-roll icon from Tupelo, Mississippi, who liked grilled peanut butter and banana sandwiches?"

"No. I'm referring to the domesticated fowl from a fertilized egg who likes fresh worms."

Aunt Zoe pulled the lid off her Betty Boop cookie jar and grabbed a couple of molasses cookies. "Here, Cornelius. Maybe one of these will sweeten up Violet."

He took the cookies, handing one to me. "Speaking of your hair," he started, looking at that very thing as he chewed on his cookie.

"We probably shouldn't." I bit into the sweet morsel,

smiling as I chewed. Aunt Zoe was right, the cookie did make me feel better.

"I recently read that blackstrap molasses diluted with water can keep your hair from turning gray and falling out."

When Cornelius wasn't trying to make ghosts talk to him, he was a walking encyclopedia of random facts—from chickens to voodoo to blackstrap molasses and more.

"It's also good for menstrual cramps and moisturizing your skin." He shoved the last of the cookie into his mouth.

Splendid, but could I use it as bait for a *lidérc*? "So, I should take daily dips in molasses?"

"Doc would probably enjoy your kisses more." Aunt Zoe grabbed another cookie and handed it to me. "You'd better have two."

Cornelius took another while she had the lid open. "Two tablespoons in your morning drink will relieve constipation, too."

I wrinkled my nose, swallowing a mouthful of molasses goodness. "You know, Cornelius, these really aren't topics you should be discussing socially. I think you've been hanging out with ghosts too much."

"On the contrary, I was visiting with your tall medium this afternoon, not the ghost next door."

My "tall medium" was what Cornelius called Doc, who went by many titles, including *das Orakel* and "Candy Cane." The former had to do with his psychic medium occupation according to the paranormal community in Deadwood, the latter was what I'd taken to calling him since the last time we were naked and alone in front of the fireplace with a spool of red ribbon left over from wrapping presents. Make that mostly naked—we hadn't wasted time stripping all of the way down, and the floor in Aunt Zoe's living room had a draft.

As for the "ghost next door," that was my old boss who'd been murdered months ago and had come back to keep an eye on her baby—Calamity Jane Realty, where I spent my days trying to make a living selling real estate.

"Where is Doc?" Aunt Zoe asked him.

"He needed to collect some appurtenances at his place of residence."

I was going to need to pour molasses in my ears if Cornelius was going to keep using words like *appurtenance* tonight.

"Did Doc ask you to join us?" I plucked a third cookie from the jar, broke it in half, and shared with my Cossack hat-wearing pal.

"There was no asking involved." He took me up on my cookie offer. "I was informed that my presence was required here and to dress appropriately."

"I thought you were flying to Australia to visit your sister." He'd told me months ago that she was Down Under trying to connect with the ghost of the notorious Ned Kelly.

"That didn't work out."

"Why not?"

"She has relocated to Nevada." Cornelius eyed me while chewing on his portion of cookie. "If you're the *real* Violet Parker, how would you go about channeling the spirit of a two-hundred-year-old French fur trapper?"

I tapped my index finger on my chin. "For starters, I'd offer to trade him your hat for some molasses."

The doorbell rang.

Reid?

Aunt Zoe's scowl returned front and center. She must have been reading my thoughts.

I escaped to the dining room, swallowing a mouthful of cookie as I opened the front door. "Where's the fire?"

It wasn't Reid.

Doc stood there, arms laden with a bottle of tequila and a six-pack of Corona, a full grocery bag, and an open-topped box full of crackers and cheese.

He eyed me up and down, smiling at what he saw. "The fire's in your pants, Boots."

It was *on* my pajamas tonight, too. I stepped back, ushering him inside.

"I've been hot and bothered all day long thinking about you and your flames." He landed a brief "Hello" kiss on my cheek as he passed, his beard stubble tickling my skin, and set the six-pack on the sideboard.

"Oh, really?" I closed the door behind him and took the bottle of tequila and the grocery bag to lighten his load. "And just what are you going to do about that overheating issue of yours?"

"I have a plan." He set the box next to the Corona and shucked his thick coat. He wore a black T-shirt with the candy cane pajama pants I'd found on sale this week and given to him as a private joke.

"Nice candy canes," I teased. "Did you bring any ribbon?"

He winked at me. "It's a New Year's surprise."

"So, does this plan of yours involve a big fire hose for my flames?"

"Maybe." He opened the hall closet door.

"Does it include a ball gag and a green, three-boobed, Area 51 love doll?"

Doc paused in the midst of hanging up his coat, looking over at me with one raised eyebrow. "*Three* breasts, you say?"

I nodded. "Big green ones." I lowered my voice for his ears only. "Harvey once told me you were a breast man."

Old Man Harvey, my rifle-toting, self-proclaimed bodyguard, was also the one who'd told me about the blowup alien love doll. I was still trying to forget the rest of his anecdote that went with that danged doll.

Doc shut the closet door, his focus aimed below my

chin. "Well, I certainly am smitten with both of yours." His gaze lifted. "And your lips, too. Now what was this about a ball gag?"

I laughed and blew him a kiss.

"That's not good enough, Killer." He caught my hand and pulled me close. "You straightened your hair."

"I did." I couldn't tell from his statement if that was a good or bad thing for him.

"What's the occasion?" He sounded like Aunt Zoe.

"Maybe I wanted to see if I liked it better." Which wasn't totally true, but I didn't want to dig into that murky bog of fears right now. I needed to stay focused on catching that damned *lidérc*.

"Do you?"

Not really. It took a lot of time and labor and I was too lazy most mornings to do much more than wet my bird's nest down and race out the door. "It's softer. What do you think?"

"It's …" he paused, sliding his fingers through it, watching it fall onto my shoulder. "Shiny and pretty."

"Why are there frown lines around your mouth then?"

He shrugged. "I like your curls and curves."

Good, because I came by both of those naturally.

His dark eyes held mine. "I like them a lot, Boots. They're a wild and sexy combination, and I fantasize about them daily."

"Daily, you say?" I batted my eyelashes at him, relieved he wasn't overly enamored by my new look.

"Sometimes hourly even," he added, leaning toward me.

I went up on my toes to meet him halfway. "Not every single minute, though?"

His focus lowered to my lips. "Well, when I'm in the shower …"

"Yeah?" I smiled, thinking fondly of him surrounded by steam.

Before we could do more than make brief lip contact, the rapid thud of footfalls came down the stairs.

"Mom?"

I tried to ignore my child and kissed Doc again.

Layne groaned at the sight of us mid-smooch. "Come on, Doc. You know she has girl cooties, right? Jett told me that once those things get inside of you, they're like tapeworms. You're doomed."

I pulled away and grimaced down at my son. *Tapeworms?* "Who's Jett?"

"He sits next to Layne in Art," Doc answered, surprising me with his knowledge about my son's classmates. He let go of me and squeezed Layne's shoulder. "Sorry, kid, but your mother's cooties took over my brain months ago. There's no hope for me now."

"No cure at all?" Layne asked, eyeing me like he could see my cooties crawling all over my face.

"Nope. I'm definitely doomed. Hey, I like your skeleton pajamas. They remind me of Natalie's Halloween costume." Doc took the grocery bag from me and handed it to Layne, along with the box. "Take those to the kitchen for me, would you?"

As Layne carried the goods away, I gave Doc a mock glare. "Doomed, huh?"

"Yeah, but I'm crazy about your cooties." Doc put his arm around my shoulder, dropping a kiss on my temple. "I hope you and Zoe don't mind that I invited Cornelius to join us. He was planning to spend the night staring at the monitors, watching for Jane to show up. I figured he needed a break from dead people."

"You think we'll be more entertaining?"

"That depends."

"On what?"

"How much tequila you drink tonight, you lush."

I tickled his ribs, making him squirm and laugh.

We'd no sooner joined Aunt Zoe, Cornelius, and Layne in the kitchen than someone knocked on the back door.

Reid waved at us as we all turned his way, smiling through the door's window.

"Violet Lynn!" Aunt Zoe said through clenched teeth.

"What's he doing here?" I played dumb.

Reid held up a bottle of wine and a big container of mixed nuts. "Happy almost New Year's!" he called through the glass.

"Oh, look. It's your favorite wine, Aunt Zoe. A Gamay." Which was exactly what I'd suggested to Reid yesterday to help smooth Aunt Zoe's ruffled feathers.

"I'm not drinking that," she said under her breath.

Layne ran over and opened the back door. "Hi, Reid! I like your fire truck pajama pants."

Reid had followed the party dress code, wearing a red thermal shirt under his canvas coat, which he slipped off and handed to Layne to hang up in the other room.

"This is a bad idea," Aunt Zoe whispered as Layne skipped past us.

"We'll all be here with you," I murmured. "What could go wrong?"

"Who knows with Reid? We don't need history to repeat itself." She huffed. "And I certainly don't like the look of his fancy nuts."

I stifled a giggle and swatted her on the shoulder. "Knock it off."

Reid's gaze settled on my aunt. He took his time checking out her silk pajamas. "You look good, Zo. I hope you don't mind me joining you tonight. Sparky mentioned that you were having a party at home and if I didn't have anything else to do, I should come over."

I held steady under Aunt Zoe's glare. "What? The poor guy was going to be all alone on New Year's Eve."

Still holding onto the container of nuts, Reid nodded to

Doc and Cornelius.

She cursed quietly and then turned back to her old flame. "Of course you're welcome." She walked over and took the bottle of wine from his hand.

Reid and I shared a victory grin.

"Set your nuts down over there." She pointed toward the table.

When Reid laughed at her choice of words, she jokingly threatened to clobber him with the wine bottle.

"You'd better watch yourself tonight," she said, placing the bottle next to the others on the counter.

"I'll be good, Zo. Just don't take your anger out on my poor nuts." He winked at me.

Doc chuckled. "There are no guarantees when it comes to Parker women. Kevlar might help, though."

"Or chain mail," Cornelius threw out, rubbing his forearm still. The big baby.

"Better your nuts than that glass jaw of yours, Martin." Aunt Zoe held her fist up, continuing her impression of the late Jackie Gleason. "Try anything funny with me while I'm drinking and I'll knock you into next year."

Chapter Three

A lot of curious things come in groups of sixes—beer, underwear, sculpted abs, cheap nail polish, even cheaper crayons, senses for the paranormally "gifted" folks like Doc and Cornelius, and New Year's Eve partiers in Aunt Zoe's warm and cozy kitchen.

We all settled in around the kitchen table with plates full of crackers, cheese, cookies, my aunt's famous lemon bars, and Reid's "fancy" nuts. Aunt Zoe took the seat to my left, keeping Cornelius between her and Reid. Doc was on my right, with Layne next to him. In the middle of the table Layne had spread out the Boo-ville board game Cornelius had brought, assigning each of us a different-colored token.

While my son worked on setting up the evening's entertainment, I stacked a piece of aged white cheddar on a buttery cracker and shoved both in my mouth at once. "This cheese is delicious," I said to Doc after I gulped it down, reaching for more.

"One of my clients gave it to me for Christmas."

Doc made a living by helping people double and triple their money, which made him well-liked by many. Me? I simply wanted him for his body ... and now his cheese, too.

I pointed a cracker at my tsar-loving, ghost-chatting pal across the table from me. "I wouldn't have pegged you for a guy who plays board games. Where'd you get this?" I'd not heard of a game called Boo-ville before.

"It appeared in my suite last Halloween." Cornelius took a sip of the wine Reid had brought. His plate was half filled with molasses cookies and the other half loaded with the finger-size lemon bars. Jeez, that was a lot of sugar. Maybe he was part ant. Or hummingbird, with the way he hummed during our séances.

"From whom?" I pressed.

"Most likely a ghost."

First a furry hat, now a board game? Where was Cornelius finding these gift-bearing ghosts? I could have used one or two of them in my life when I was single and lonely, especially around Valentine's Day. And how come he got all of the cool presents from the ectoplasmic crowd? All I'd been offered so far from the ghosts I'd met were a half-burnt clown doll, an invitation to a creepy tea party, and one of my co-workers' freshly ripped-out canine teeth. Talk about crappy white elephant gifts.

"It looks a little bit like the game Clue," Aunt Zoe said, her head cocked while reading the names on the board. "Only instead of the conservatory and the library and other rooms in the regular game, there's a police station, court house, hospital, school, and prison, to name a few. All rundown and haunted, too, from the looks of them."

Reid chuckled. "Sparky would fit right in at Boo-ville."

"They'd probably elect her as mayor," Doc added, faking shock when I stole a piece of gouda cheese from his plate as punishment.

I grabbed another cracker for the stolen piece of cheese. "Poke fun, you two, but I'd advise you to keep one eye open when you sleep tonight, or you might find yourself with a reverse Mohawk come morning light."

"That veiled threat is very Aries of you," Cornelius said. "It's pulsing with passion."

I threw the cracker at him Frisbee-style, but it landed on Aunt Zoe's arm. "Shove that up your pulsing *ass*-trology."

"Language, Mom," Layne chastised.

"That didn't even make sense, Violet Lynn." Aunt Zoe ate the makeshift Frisbee.

Doc handed me another cracker. "I like it when you pulse, Tiger."

"That sounds like something a person with brain cooties would say," Layne grumbled, which made Doc laugh and tousle the kid's hair. "Why do you call my mom 'Tiger'?"

My cheeks warmed at the heated look Doc sent my way.

"Because she growls a lot," he answered, his fingers flirting their way up my inseam under the table.

"Which is also very Aries of her," Cornelius said, his cornflower blue eyes twinkling when I growled across the table at him.

"Who are the people on the cards?" Aunt Zoe asked Layne, drawing our focus back to the game.

He pushed the cards her way and then scanned the instructions. "Let's see, there should be six."

Once again, the number six came into play. It had to be my lucky number tonight.

"Alcatraz Al," Layne read. "Amityville Amy, Deadwood Daisy, LaLaurie Lou, Rolling Hills Harry, and Winchester Wendy."

"Those are odd names," I said around a mouthful of cheese and crumbs.

Cornelius picked up one of the cards, inspecting it. "On the contrary, they make complete sense."

"In what world? Alice in Wonderland?"

"They're all haunted locations," Doc answered because Cornelius was busy stuffing his pie hole with a lemon bar.

"Amityville and Alcatraz, I know," Reid said, checking out the people cards, too. "And Deadwood, of course."

I brushed cracker crumbs from my cheeks. "But what's LaLaurie and Rolling Hills?"

"LaLaurie refers to Madame Delphine LaLaurie's mansion in New Orleans," Cornelius said. He'd spent much of his childhood down in Louisiana with his grandmother, a well-known seer. Was she also the one he'd said was some sort of voodoo queen in the swamplands?

"So, it's a haunted mansion?" Reid reached for his glass of Aunt Zoe's famous whiskey slush that was mixed with lemon-lime soda pop. "Did this LaLaurie house give Walt Disney the idea for his spooky mansion in Disneyland?"

Cornelius shook his head. "From what I've read, the original engineers at the theme park based the setting for the old mansion off various plantation homes around New Orleans. However, Disney himself was a fan of the Winchester Mystery House and all of its eccentricities."

"That explains the Winchester Wendy card," I said, getting up to refill my drink. "What's the story behind Rolling Hills Harry?"

"It's the Rolling Hills Asylum in Bethany, New York," Doc explained. "Will you make me one of those … what do you call them?"

"Salty Chihuahua," I said, grabbing another glass from the cupboard. It was basically tequila and Aunt Zoe's lemonade with a squeeze of lime and a salty rim, but the name made it sound more exciting.

"A haunted asylum would be creepy," Aunt Zoe said.

So was a haunted opera house, especially when a spiky killer was stalking me in the dark. I glanced Aunt Zoe's way as I dipped the glasses in kosher salt, watching her gather the cards together and slide them back to Layne.

"It is quite spine-chilling in reality." Cornelius joined me at the counter, pouring more wine into his glass and grabbing a couple more lemon bars. "The administrators at Rolling Hills were fans of electroshock therapy and lobotomies, and several of the dead inmates are still perturbed about their treatment there."

I shuddered at the idea of running into an insane ghost. Oh, wait, I already had multiple times, along with her twisted, sinister mother. Just the thought of little Wilda Hessler made my knees feel rubbery. She was right up there on the "Scary-as-Hell" scale next to the *lidérc*. Too bad I couldn't take them both out at the same time.

My hand trembled when I poured the tequila into the glass of lemonade. Damn it, I needed to nut up and stop being such a wuss about facing off with my demons. Although to be fair, when people usually talked about their "demons," they weren't actual orange-eyed, pustule-covered beings that ripped their own faces off, nor could their demons slice them to pieces in the dark like mine could.

"What's the object of this game, Layne?" Doc asked, his deep voice bringing me back to the safe and comfortable present.

"We're supposed to figure out who caught the ghost in which building with which paranormal investigator tool."

This board game was right up Cornelius's alley. Who was his mystery gift giver? A fellow investigator? Maybe I could learn a thing or two tonight for the next time he roped me into participating in one of his paranormal parties.

As I returned to the table with two drinks in hand, Layne grabbed a velvet pouch from the box and dumped its contents onto the center of the board.

We all leaned forward to check out the tools—except for Cornelius, who was busy making a lemon bar sandwich between two molasses cookies.

I counted six tools. Hmmmm. Six again.

"What are these?" Reid asked, picking up a small cone with what looked like a weird spaceship on the top.

"Let's see," Layne said, kneeling on his chair for better tabletop leverage. He held the paper instructions up next to the cone piece. "The one you're holding is an audio recorder with a 360-degree microphone to pick up ghost chatter." He grabbed up another game piece and held it in front of the instructions. "This one here is a parascope. It detects a static field."

"So it'd go haywire in the dryer?" I joked.

Aunt Zoe groaned. "That joke wasn't half bad, Violet—it was 100 percent bad."

"What's important about static fields?" Layne asked.

"Static fields are better than magnetic fields." Cornelius took another bite of his cookie-bar sandwich.

Layne looked from Cornelius to Doc. "Why?"

"Magnetic fields are used in a lot of everyday technology," Doc explained, draping his arm over the back of my chair. "That means they can cause false meter readings when trying to detect ghosts. Static fields are natural DC electric fields found on humans and objects. A static field meter like a parascope will give you a more accurate reading of your ghostly company."

Layne nodded, apparently understanding more than I did about magnetic and static fields. Then again, he wasn't on his second Salty Chihuahua, so he had a leg up on me.

Cornelius picked up another game piece. "And this one is a helmet with an attached infrared camera."

"IR cameras detect infrared energy," Doc explained to us.

"And that helps me catch a ghost how?" I asked.

"They use infrared radiation to create an image from temperature variations. The fluctuations and differences in temperature can indicate the presence of an apparition. Some think the colder the anomaly, the more likely it is a ghost."

"We use something like that at work," Reid murmured, taking the IR camera piece from Cornelius.

I grimaced at the idea of walking through a haunted building with an IR camera. These days, I wasn't sure I wanted to know what entities were in a room with me. Ghosts like Prudence, my Executioner predecessor who'd been haunting a house up in Lead for over a century, and little Wilda Hessler gave me hives without even being able to see them.

"What's the walkie-talkie looking dealio?" I asked.

"That's a Mel meter," Cornelius answered before Layne read aloud about it. "It measures EMF and temperature."

"EMF as in electromagnetic field?" Reid asked, handing the IR camera piece to Aunt Zoe. I noticed his hand touched hers long enough to rouse a dirty look from her before she snatched the piece away.

"Right," Doc answered Reid's question. "It measures EMF fluctuations, which many believe ghosts have the ability to manipulate."

Aunt Zoe held up another investigator tool. "What's this tripod with the little TV screen on it?"

Layne read from the paper. "An SLS camera."

"A Kinect SLS camera," Cornelius specified. "It's used to detect entities that can't be seen with the naked eye."

"So, it displays them on the screen?" Inspired by Cornelius, I grabbed two pieces of cheese and slid a cracker between them, making a cracker sandwich.

"Yes." Doc stole my mini-sandwich. "But they look like stick figures, not Casper." He popped his pilfered treasure into his mouth.

"Brat." I pinched his side, making him grunt and lean away from me.

Layne's hazel eyes widened. "How cool would it be to see a real ghost?"

Doc and I exchanged knowing looks. Not very cool at all. More like heart-stopping, especially in a haunted house or hotel.

"This looks like an old radio," Reid said, holding up the last ghost-hunting tool.

"It's a Poltercom," Cornelius said, his cookie-bar sandwich now history. He lifted his glass of wine, holding the glass up to the light and peering into the dark red liquid. "Sort of reminds me of drinking blood."

Knowing Cornelius as I did, I wouldn't blink twice if he told me he had blood for dinner every other night.

"Maybe we should start calling you Count Cornelius," I said, taking a salty-sweet sip of my drink.

"A polter-what?" Reid asked, still inspecting the game piece.

"It's a spirit box used to communicate with ghosts," Doc told him, his fingers toying with my hair. "You turn the knob, rolling back and forth through the stations, picking up tidbits of ghostly conversations."

That reminded me of the night we were in the attic at Galena House with Cooper and Cornelius. There'd been an unplugged old radio up there with us. Thankfully, I hadn't heard any ghostly chatter coming from it, though, only golden oldies. I might have peed my pants otherwise.

"Are we ready to play?" Layne asked, mixing the cards. After a group agreement, he tucked away the three winning cards and handed out the rest around the table.

"Layne," Aunt Zoe said after all cards were dealt. "Before we start, will you go shut off the television and turn on the stereo. We could use background music for this game."

As soon as Layne ran out of the room, I turned to my aunt. "It's too bad there isn't a game for how to catch a *lidérc*, including which tool to use for the job. I could really use some ideas on how to lasso that smoky sucker."

Reid eyed me, a rare frown on his face. "Don't tell me you're going after that asshole again."

"I have to."

Aunt Zoe harrumphed. "No, you don't."

"Yes, I do, and I'm done arguing whether I should or

should not." I rested my elbows on the table. "What I need from you guys is help figuring out how to catch it. I don't think I can do this on my own—the figuring-out part, I mean. The catching part will need to be a solo job."

"Not solo," Doc said, his voice stern.

"Doc," I started.

He held up his hand. "We're a team. End of discussion."

"What exactly is a *lidérc*?" Cornelius asked.

The noise from the TV in the living room quieted.

"A parasite," Aunt Zoe told him quietly. "It will attach itself to you mentally and slowly suck the life from you. And when you're no longer breathing, it will steal your soul."

"That reminds me of a voodoo priest my grandmother told me about. What does it do with these commandeered souls?"

"According to mythology sources I've read, it adds them to its macabre collection to be used when it likes for whatever dark purpose. An eternity of servitude, in other words."

"It's a trickster," Reid spoke up, stirring the whiskey slush in his glass. "It will dig into your thoughts and make you believe your dead loved ones have returned."

Reid had experienced the Hungarian devil's mind game firsthand a month ago when it took on the image of his father in order to lure him closer. Fortunately, I was there to keep it from latching onto him. Okay, so maybe I might have dangled him out there as bait first, which wasn't one of my brighter ideas, but in the end the *lidérc* hadn't won and Reid was still a plain ol' guy on a mission to win back my aunt's heart. No harm, no foul.

And no attached parasitic devil, either.

"It also preys on loneliness," Doc told Cornelius, his low volume matching Zoe's. "Some legends talk of it being a shape-shifting demon that takes on three forms. The first being an incubus demon that often appears as an absent lover, or a dead spouse or well-loved family member. It will fill the void in the victim's life, which seems great at first but eventually causes the victim to waste away."

The sound of a guitar filtered in from the living room, followed by the Doobie Brothers crooning about building a raft and floating on some black water.

"The second shape it takes is a featherless chicken with one goose leg and a human foot," Doc continued. "After it enters your home, it can never be banished. If you don't keep it busy with tasks, it will destroy those who live there."

"And the third?" Reid asked.

"A death omen light." Doc paused to take a sip of his drink. "It's like a glowing ball that hovers over a house until someone inside dies."

Layne walked into the room as Doc finished. "What are you guys talking about?"

"Nothing," I lied, wanting to shield him from my troubles.

"Your nose is twitching, Mom."

Son of a peach pit! My kid knew my tells too well. Layne had studied up on interrogation skills a couple of months ago and ever since then he had watched me like Columbo hot on a crook's tail.

Doc whispered next to my ear, "You're in trouble now, Tiger."

Layne settled into his chair as "Black Water" really got rolling on the stereo. "It sounded like Doc was talking about a *lidérc*," he said and picked up his cards.

Everyone stilled, all eyes on Layne.

"What do you know about a *lidérc*?" Doc asked him.

"When I read that book I found in Mom's room about all those women gladiators," he said, shooting me a guilty glance. "There were a couple stories that talked about battling a *lidérc*, so I looked it up on the computer in the library."

I shifted in my seat, not liking my kid being this close to the fire.

Doc squeezed my shoulder. "What did I forget about the *lidérc*?" he asked Layne.

"You didn't mention that it's been described as a tiny devil found in old clothes or glass bottles. Whoever owns this type of *lidérc* becomes super rich because the creature owns their soul. Oh, and they can also do super feats. Kind of reminds me of Superman, only if he was a bad guy instead of good."

Super feats? Criminy! Why couldn't I have to take down a garden gnome?

"How many times did you read that book?" I asked.

He shrugged, staring extra intently at the cards in his hand. "Maybe a couple."

"Layne Alan," I warned. He wasn't the only one who could sniff out a fibber.

"Okay, a few times. But I couldn't help it, Mom. It had some really cool weapons in it and the stories to go with them."

"Layne," Doc cut in. "In the stories you read about the gladiators, did any of them have a weapon that could possibly defeat a *lidérc*?"

Layne lowered his cards, his forehead wrinkling. After a few beats, he shook his head. "I don't think so."

Shit. Back to square one—how to catch a damned *lidérc*.

I raised my glass in a mock toast to Aunt Zoe. "Let the games begin."

Chapter Four

The first game was a learning one. It took some time getting used to the players' names, the investigating doohickeys they used, and the haunted buildings. Layne won the round, guessing LaLaurie Lou found an "old peg-legged sailor ghost" in the haunted hospital with the parascope.

"Old peg-legged sailor?" I handed him my cards to mix up with the others. "Who said anything about the ghost being a sailor?"

Layne shrugged. "I was just thinking of a joke I heard."

"Let's hear it." Doc grabbed my empty glass along with his. "You want another?"

I nodded, pinching my lower lip. It wasn't even a smidgeon numb yet, but with three hours until midnight, I'd need to sip the next drink.

He collected Aunt Zoe's glass on his way to the counter, too, taking her order.

Layne cleared his throat. "An old sailor walks into a bar with a ship's wheel stuffed down the front of his pants. The bartender says, 'You have a wheel in your pants.' The sailor says, 'I know, and it's driving me nuts.' " He delivered the punch line in a high-pitched voice, sounding like a wee leprechaun looking for "me Lucky Charms" instead of a crusty sailor.

Reid and Doc laughed outright. A crooked smile sat on

Cornelius' lips, which was his version of a chuckle.

Aunt Zoe and I exchanged groans. "Where on earth did you hear that joke, child?" she asked.

I had a feeling it was compliments of either Natalie, who had a vast repertoire of bawdy jokes, or Harvey, who was a plain old dirty bird.

"Harvey told it to me at Christmas." Layne separated out the cards per people, places, and paranormal tools, and then mixed each of the category groups. "He said that when he was growing up, his grandpappy used to share sips of something called 'hooch' with him and tell all sorts of jokes like that one while they were waiting for Christmas dinner to be ready."

Of course. What was Christmas without swigs of homemade hooch and jokes about a sailor's nuts? My family's tradition of stringing popcorn while watching Santa Claus movies would have bored Harvey to sleep.

Doc set another tequila-lemonade in front of me. "There's a tad more Chihuahua in that one for you." He pointed at my plate. "You want me to grab more snacks while I'm up?"

"Yes. Some of that gouda cheese and crackers, please."

As Doc returned to the counter, Cornelius tossed a cookie my way. "You should probably eat more molasses if you're going to keep eating cheese."

When I scowled at him, he added, "It's a natural lax—"

"*Nyet!*"

He pointed a bony finger at me. "Now you're speaking Russian. My earlier suspicion was on the mark."

Doc set my plate of cheese and crackers in front of me. "What suspicion?"

"He thinks I'm not me."

"Who are you, then?" Reid pushed his chair back and stood, stretching his back.

"A malevolent doppelganger."

Doc's thigh bumped mine as he settled in at the table again. I bumped him back, earning a warm smile in return. Even though we'd been together for a few months now, I still reveled in the small touches that passed between us. The lack of physical contact from someone other than my kids for most of the last decade was one of the loneliest aspects of being single for me. I'd pined for that part of a relationship even more than sex … and boy oh boy, had I missed sex.

"And this malevolent harbinger of bad luck theory is based on what?" Doc asked.

"My straightened hair." I tried to wrap a strand around my finger, but without my usual curls, it was slippery. "Cornelius doesn't trust it."

"I think you look very pretty, Mom."

"Thank you, Layne." I pulled the cards he dealt me closer. "You've always been my favorite son."

He sniffed. "I'm your only son."

"That, too."

Cornelius peered at my hair over his cards, his dark eyebrows wavy. "Your hair is making me sweaty."

That didn't even make any sense. I organized my cards, fighting the urge to throw one of my slippers at him. "If you're sweaty, it's because you're still wearing that furry hat. You're no longer in Siberia, Boris."

"It's too straight," he continued as if I hadn't spoken. "I'm having trouble concentrating on the game."

"You've eaten a butt load of sugar tonight," I returned, noting on my scrap paper what cards I held. "It's a wonder you haven't keeled over in a diabetic coma."

"My heart keeps fluttering every time I look at it."

I threw down my cards. "It's just a freaking hairdo, you big skinny turkey."

"That's not necessarily true," Aunt Zoe weighed in, taking a sip of the whiskey slush Doc had made for her.

Oh, jeez. Not this again. "Oh, really, Dr. Freud?"

"Really, Cleopatra, you beautiful Queen of Denial." She lowered her cards. "I think you're struggling with your identity and your future. Straightening your hair is evidence of this battle with insecurities."

I guffawed, turning to Doc, expecting to find him rolling his eyes along with me.

He wasn't.

"Don't tell me you're buying Aunt Zoe's snake oil."

His gaze drifted to my straight ends. "What exactly were you thinking when you decided to straighten your hair today?"

"Uhhhh …" My cheeks warmed.

Truth be told, one of the things I was thinking was that he might find me sexier with straight hair because it would make me seem like I had my shit together. But I'd sooner ring in the New Year with Wilda and her scream-inspiring mother than admit that truth in front of this audience.

"Well." I toyed with the pencil I was using for taking game notes. "Maybe I thought it would be a fun changeup." That was partially true.

"A changeup from what, though?" Aunt Zoe pressed.

"I don't know, the same old chaotic and unruly curls."

"Uh huh." Aunt Zoe nodded knowingly. "This relates to our earlier *game*." She shot a tight frown in Layne's direction. "You know, Violet, the role-playing game we were discussing that involves the book of female gladiators Layne read and you didn't?"

I crossed my arms. "I was sick at the time."

"And what's been your excuse since then?"

"I've been a little busy." When Aunt Zoe stared at me, apparently unimpressed with my excuse, I pointed my thumb toward the guy next to me. "It's Doc's fault."

Reid laughed, dropping into his chair. His small glass of plain whiskey no longer had the "slush" part.

The accused party sitting next to me let out a scoff. "After I showered you with cheese and tequila, you throw me under the bus."

Cornelius leaned back, studying me as though I were green with three boobs. "Aries do tend to have a weakness of being self-centered, often speaking without thinking."

"Would you cram it with this Aries bullshi—" I remembered my nine-year-old's ears at the last second. "Crapola."

"What does Violet wanting to straighten her hair have to do with the book on female gladiators?" Reid asked as he scanned his cards.

Zoe's mouth tightened for a moment. She sent a wrinkled brow in Layne's direction. "Well, when Violet and I were discussing the life of a gladiator, she questioned if she'd have the gumption to be as strong as one of those women—mentally, not physically."

Physically, too. Those women probably looked like Conan the Barbarian's sisters, especially if they were swinging swords around day and night. Hell, I struggled with holding onto an umbrella on a windy day.

"You think Sparky changed her hairstyle to raise her self-confidence?" Reid asked.

"Possibly. It might be a matter of trying to *look* the part of a warrior so that she could *feel* more like a warrior mentally."

"Ah hah." Cornelius tapped his long fingers together. "She's wearing a helmet into battle. That explains my anxiety. I'm experiencing pre-war jitters due to her hair."

What a bunch of psychological mumbo-jumbo. I took a sip of my drink, needing something to take the edge off this topic. The tequila heated my throat this time. Doc hadn't been kidding about the extra "Chihuahua" in it. *Ay yi yi.*

"Your conjecture would offer a reasonable explanation for the hairstyle change," Doc said to Aunt Zoe.

Grrrr. Not him, too.

"Come on, you guys." A search around the table found all eyes on me, including Layne's. Now I knew what bacteria grown in a petri dish felt like. I scrubbed my hands down my face. "It's only hair, that's all. You're making something out of nothing."

"Are we, though?" Aunt Zoe asked.

"You're speaking in strange tongues tonight," Cornelius reminded me.

"That's your silly hat's fault." I wrinkled my nose at him. "How about I come over there and pinch you again? Will that be more normal for you?"

"Make that out of character aside from your usual aggressive Aries tendencies, that is."

If he didn't knock off this astrology baloney, I was going to shove my Aries tendencies along with that damned hat of his where the sun didn't shine and the nights were dark and humid.

"I think you could be one of those female gladiators, Mom." Layne shook the dice in his hands. Since he'd won the last game, he got to go first. "You can be really tough when I forget to put the toilet seat down or blow up a doghouse."

"I'm not sure those examples are helping my cause, Layne."

He rolled two sixes. "Yes!" He pumped his fist and moved his token into the haunted fire station.

"I agree with Layne," Reid said, giving me a thumbs-up. "And don't forget you're an ace fire-starter, Sparky."

I pointed a piece of cheese at him. "None of those blazes were my fault."

"You're hell on wheels, Tiger," Doc said, joining my cheering squad. "Nothing you do on the outside will change what you are on the inside."

"Yeah, but what's on the inside often has me wanting to

pack up the kids and move to the South Pole. If," I paused, glancing pointedly at Layne, who was busy scanning his cards as he prepped to make the first guess of the new round. "And we're still only role playing here, you guys. But if I were to have to hunt a *lidérc* like some of those women in Aunt Zoe's book, how would I go about starting that task? Short of a butterfly net …" *or a war hammer*, which I'd failed with last time I faced off with the damned devil. "How would I catch and bag the devil?"

Silence greeted me.

That was what I thought. We were heading into unchartered forests here, where unknown assassins skulked in the deep shadows.

Layne looked up from his cards, his forehead lined. "You can't outrun this, Mom."

Was he talking about the *lidérc* or something more philosophical, such as my apparently obvious self-confidence issues? I tried to lighten the atmosphere. "Outrun what, sweetie? You mean the ice cream truck?"

"The *lidérc*," he said, all serious-faced. "From what I read about it in a myths and legends book at the library, the *lidérc* moves like the wind."

More like smoke in the wind, a fact I'd witnessed firsthand the last time I tried to take out the Hungarian devil.

I blew out a breath, trying to hide my qualms behind a smile that wouldn't scare young children away or turn anyone at the table into a pillar of salt.

"So, we all agree that *if* I were one of those female gladiators in the book, running from a *lidérc* would not be an option."

That meant I'd need to face it head-on.

Chapter Five

My hippie mother preferred to view life through nearsighted, rose-colored glasses. While I was growing up, she oozed flower-child positivity at almost every turn, often to the point of making my dad rant and rave at the same moon and stars of which she spoke so highly.

For example, when my brother broke his arm trying to fly with cardboard wings out of his friend's tree fort, Mom cooed about how wonderful it was that Quint was living out his imagination rather than wallowing in his past. What sort of "past" an eight-year-old boy living in boring suburbia might have experienced that would inspire a flying leap out of a tree was beyond my father and me to this day.

Then there was the time Susan, my evil little sister whom I still lovingly call the Bride of Satan, decapitated my favorite baby doll, filled its torso with sugar ants, and glued the head back in place. That evening, while Mom was trying to wash the ants out of my hair for the third time, she told me, "Always remember, Violet, the greater your storm, the bigger and more beautiful your rainbow."

Tonight, as I sat at the kitchen table watching my fellow partiers take turns rolling the dice while trying to catch a slippery ghost in Boo-ville, I pondered how my mom would spin my current *lidérc* conundrum. What would she say to make me feel better about snagging a super-speedy parasitic entity that no known weapon could destroy?

Probably something that would inspire a forehead slap, like one of her favorites—*Every problem has a solution, Violet.*

Blah! How many times had I heard that one from her? She'd cited it repeatedly after I found out I was pregnant with twins, and the sperm donor had up and skipped town after extracting his philandering penis from the Bride of Satan's vagina.

Let your past make you better, Violet, not bitter.

Whatever, Mother. I drew unhappy faces on the back of my game scrap sheet.

But the mother-mimicking voice in my head was right—enough about Susan, who was currently down on some Caribbean island fixing the gigantic fuckup she'd created by stealing my identity and marrying me off to a now-dead millionaire. Maybe, with the help of my family history book and an infusion of my mother's endless positivity, I could come up with at least one viable solution.

Or this all could be the Salty Chihuahua talking.

I took another sip of my drink in case it wasn't.

Now where was I? Oh, according to my son's memory of what he'd read in our family history book, no weapons worked against a *lidérc*, nor was I going to be able to outrun the son of a gun. That left me in a bit of a pickle.

"Layne." I sat forward, resting my elbows on the table. "Do you remember that gladiator who let a *lidérc* attach to her?"

His hazel eyes met mine. "You mean that one who jumped off a cliff?"

And then died, yes. Unfortunately for the Executioner, Aunt Zoe didn't think her suicidal jump off the cliff eliminated the Hungarian asshole. Her death had set it free instead.

"Yes, that one." I laced my fingers together, wondering how much I should talk about this with my son. I didn't want to give him nightmares. Then again, the kid had read the family book more than once. He might end up giving *me* nightmares. "Did you read anything about how the gladiator managed to catch it?"

"She didn't 'catch' it, Violet," Aunt Zoe said. "It attached to her."

So, if the host dies via suicide, did the *lidérc* still have control of her soul after all was said and done? Or did it take time for the devil to get its claws sunk into its victim?

I pulled back from that temporary derailment and returned to the track I was originally following. "I know she didn't catch it per se, but was she hunting the *lidérc* when it attached to her? Or was she searching for something else at the time and ended up with the big tick stuck to her by accident?"

"Why does that matter?" Reid asked, taking the dice from Cornelius.

"I believe Violet's trying to determine if a certain method of capture was used with the *lidérc* in that particular story," Doc explained. "And if so, what technique the gladiator used."

Reid rolled the dice, moving his token into the haunted courthouse. After a glance at his notes, he guessed, "Alcatraz Al captured the pants-less ghost in the courthouse with this doohickey." He held up the old radio-like piece.

"The Poltercom," Cornelius said.

"Pants-less ghost?" Aunt Zoe asked, her eyes twinkling. "You starting to feel that whiskey there, hose jockey?"

"A little, but I'm just following in Layne's boot prints."

"What do you mean?" Layne asked.

Reid's mustache twitched. "What kind of pants do ghosts wear?" When nobody spoke up, he answered his own question. "Boo jeans."

"Oh, boo back at you," Aunt Zoe said, wrinkling her nose at him.

Layne giggled as he showed Reid a card that proved his guess wrong. "Good one, Reid."

"And if his boo jeans are dirty," Reid continued, handing Layne the dice, "he'll just wear his paranormal trousers."

Groans spread around the table, except for my son, whose grin widened. "You're funny, Reid."

"Oh, he's a real scream," Aunt Zoe said, shaking her head with a smile on her face.

"Now, Zo," Reid teased. "Don't go telling our secrets from when we were dating."

Her cheeks darkened, her smile flipping into a scowl.

"Aunt Zoe was your girlfriend once?" Layne asked, shaking the dice in his cupped hands.

"Yep." Reid raised his whiskey glass, taking a sip while watching Aunt Zoe over the rim. I could feel the heat in his gaze clear across the table. "I was a lucky guy back then."

"Are you her boyfriend now?" My son appeared to be oblivious to the sudden sparks flying in the air between the old flames as he rolled the dice.

I wasn't. "That's none of your beeswax, Layne." Squirming in my seat, I changed the subject before Aunt Zoe went looking for her shotgun to pepper Reid's flirty ass with rock salt. "Back to that gladiator with the *lidérc* stuck to her."

Doc swirled his drink while watching Layne. "If memory serves me right, that particular gladiator had not set out to catch the *lidérc*."

"Oh, yeah," Layne joined in. "She was hunting something else ... what was it?" He closed one eye and puckered his lips in thought.

"A forest-dwelling troll gone rogue," Doc supplied.

"Rogue?" I asked.

He nodded. "Turned man-eater."

I squeezed the bridge of my nose. This shit was surreal. I'd need a truck full of tequila if I had to face off with rogue trolls.

"That's right," Layne said, moving his token three spaces, unable to reach a haunted location this roll. He turned to me, his eyes lit with excitement. "The troll sicced the *lidérc* on the gladiator when they were in battle."

Doc rolled the dice. "Apparently, it was keeping the *lidérc* as a guard dog of sorts."

The *lidérc* I needed to find had been caged inside a building like a guard dog as well.

"So, she was unprepared for the attack," I said, worrying my thumbnail about a new problem I hadn't figured on—multiple attacks at once. Shit-criminy. I had enough trouble most days fighting off a mosquito.

"The gladiator was fighting solo with nobody around to help her," Doc said, his meaning clear in his narrowed gaze. "Hypothetically, if you were one of these gladiators, you would be smarter than that and go in with backup."

"Backup" as in Doc, Cooper, Cornelius, Aunt Zoe, Natalie, Harvey, and Bessie, Harvey's shotgun tagging along to cover my ass. But putting those I loved at risk—well, "loved" was stretching it for Cooper and his pokey badge—made me queasy.

Doc moved his token along the streets of Boo-ville, aiming for the haunted post office but falling two spaces short.

When he handed me the dice, I frowned down at the board. "Maybe there's some kind of body armor that would keep a *lidérc* from attaching."

"Like chain mail," Layne said, echoing Cornelius's earlier suggestion for defense against Parker women. "I bet you'd make an awesome knight, Mom."

"Or a voodoo spell," Cornelius mumbled, his mouth full with yet another cookie.

"Where are you putting all of those cookies?" I asked and rolled the dice.

"Maybe some special charms would help," Reid said, darting a heated glance in Aunt Zoe's direction.

She frowned without looking his way. "Charms are no match for a *lidérc*. They'll expose it, but won't repel it."

She'd used little bunches of birch twigs to keep it at bay back in November until I could make a run at it with my war hammer. Unfortunately, it had slipped away through the wall and taken my war hammer with it that time.

"Layne," I said. "Will you move me into the haunted police station?"

Reid chuckled. "Somebody call Coop. Violet's sneaking

around his back door."

"Well, slap me with bread and call me a sandwich," Doc said, using one of Harvey's expressions. He grinned at me. "I never thought I'd see the day when Violet would willingly walk into a police station without a warrant for her arrest." He looked over at Cornelius. "I think you're right—this is a false Violet. I wonder where the real one is hiding."

I stuck out my tongue at him. "I'll slap you with something, wiseacre."

"What's your guess, doppelganger?" Cornelius asked.

"Deadwood Daisy caught the ghost in the haunted police station using a Mel meter with absolutely no help from a single cop or a lousy detective because they were all too busy cramming doughnuts in their mouths and wrongly accusing innocent single mothers of crimes they never committed." If I hadn't run out of breath, I could have kept going on that soapbox.

Reid burst out laughing.

Doc wrapped his arm around my shoulder and pulled me into a side hug. "Don't worry, my little Deadwood Daisy. I'll bail you out every time."

Aunt Zoe reached over and patted my hand, and then slipped me one of her cards. It had the Mel meter on it. "Take a breath, dear, before you faint."

"We need to go visit that haunted jail cell," Cornelius said, pointing his empty wine glass at me.

"I cannot emphasize how much I do not want to visit anyone anywhere near a jail cell, dead or alive."

I handed the dice to Aunt Zoe. "Tell me about the twins you mentioned earlier."

"The twin gladiators who died fighting the same *lidérc* at different times?" Layne intervened.

As much as I appreciated Layne's love of learning, I wished he wasn't so good at retaining what he read some days. "Yes, those two."

"What do you want to know?" Aunt Zoe asked.

"Were they purposely hunting the *lidérc*?"

"The first one who died was. The other twin was seeking revenge."

"So they both were able to find it, though." That was the first obstacle to overcome on my hunt—where in the hell the damned devil was hiding.

"Yes." Aunt Zoe rolled, moving her token four spaces along the street next to the haunted hotel. "There were a few key things they looked for in their search for it."

Really? My pulse picked up speed. Now we were making headway with this devil hunt. "What things?"

Her forehead wrinkled as she held out the dice for Cornelius. "I can't remember. I'll go get the book." She pushed back her chair. "Play without me."

"It's more fun to play with you," Reid said under his breath.

She pointed at him. "Keep it up, Martin, and I'll gag and hog-tie you to the couch in my office."

His eyes lit up. "Zo! Such lewd talk in front of your family and friends."

Aunt Zoe grumbled something about needing her shotgun and stalked out of the room.

Reid winked at me. "She's so dang adorable when she gets all fired up."

My fingers were crossed she'd only return with the family book and not her shotgun. "You're going to have a backside full of rock salt if you're not careful."

He rubbed his hands together. "Hoo-ha! I'll take that gamble."

Cornelius tossed the dice on the table, moving his token toward the haunted cemetery. He glanced at me. "Maybe a *lidérc* could be found in the dark."

Doc made an unhappy sound in his throat.

"You mean at night?" Layne asked, watching as Reid

rolled and moved his token three spaces.

Actually, he meant in a different dark. One that Doc, Cornelius, and I had dabbled in earlier this month when we'd merged our minds and skills together. A vast blackness where spine-chilling troublemakers roamed and ruled, including a certain demon who knew me by name.

"Yes, Layne. I believe Aunt Zoe told me before that a *lidérc* is easier to find in the dark." That was the truth. When we'd gone in search of it in the Sugarloaf building, she'd wanted us to go at night because she thought we'd have better luck. And she was right.

Layne looked my way as he picked up the dice and shook them, his forehead dimpled. "I don't think it can go far, Mom."

"What do you mean?"

"I just remembered that there was a note scribbled next to the story with the gladiator who jumped off the cliff. It said the *lidérc* can't move very far without a host."

"So, it has to catch a ride on someone who travels if it wants to relocate." Out of the Black Hills, I meant, but didn't say. If it had left the Hills, I would never find it.

Traveling on a human was what it had done with Otto Sugarloaf, the doctor who'd ended up being its host after trying to rescue a young girl from the *lidérc's* hold back in their home country of Hungary. Unfortunately, the girl died when he tried to free her, and Otto gained a hitchhiker for his trip across the big pond to Lead. The *lidérc* had stayed with him until he passed. Then, somehow, Dominick—or someone else—had been able to cage it inside the Sugarloaf building, which had been Otto's home, using several cryptic restraining symbols on the walls, ceiling, and floor. That was where the Hungarian devil had stayed until a spiky bitch had freed it by tricking a silly woman seeking immortality.

"I would think it'd stick around," Doc said, watching

Layne move his token along Boo-ville's street. In other words, he believed the *lidérc* was still in the Black Hills.

"Why wouldn't it leave?" Reid asked.

Doc shrugged, picking up the dice. "Well, if there were powerful potential hosts in the same vicinity, such as one of these gladiators in the book, then I would expect it to want to lock onto a host that could withstand its succubus nature longer." He bumped my leg under the table. "Or maybe it's a vengeful devil and has an ax to grind with its jailer."

Doc's suggestion went along with something Prudence had told me when I'd asked her how to catch a *lidérc*. She'd suggested using bait to lure it, specifically, the one who'd locked it away for so long.

I heard the stairs creak under Aunt Zoe's feet as Doc rolled the dice. He moved his token past the haunted post office toward the fire station.

"I found something in a side note that I must have missed when I was translating," she said, carrying the old family book into the kitchen. She sat down and opened it to a page where she'd been using her finger as a bookmark, slipping on her reading glasses. "It says here that the first twin looked for certain clues in a host when seeking the *lidérc*." She ran her finger down the page. "Three key signs will betray a *lidérc*. First, the host's eyes no longer reflect light."

"What does that mean?" Reid asked.

"When you look into the eyes," Cornelius said, "it's like staring down into a mine shaft." He spoke as if he'd experienced that sight firsthand.

I had too the night I'd faced off with the *lidérc* in Lead. It'd been hiding behind the form of my great-grandmother, the *magistra* in our line prior to Aunt Zoe taking on the role. The old woman had often scared the bejesus out of me when I was a child.

That night in the Sugarloaf building, my great-grandmother's eyes had filled with an empty blackness for a second or two when it was trying to lure me closer for a parasitic hug. In that moment, I caught a glimpse of the Hungarian devil hiding behind the mask.

"Second, the host's breath will smell of death."

That was true also of the *lidérc* itself sans a host. The smell of rotted carcasses when it was near me had left me gagging. Interestingly, however, neither Doc, nor Aunt Zoe, nor Reid had been able to smell the sucker—or hear it. From the first floor, it'd sounded like a horse clomping across the ceiling, which had matched Aunt Zoe's comment that the *lidérc* supposedly had hooves for feet.

"One could deduce that the stench is the human host rotting on the inside," Cornelius said.

I glanced at Layne to see if this topic needed to be whitewashed with something less death-oriented. He was sucking down root beer through a straw, his focus on his game sheet. I kept forgetting that he'd already read this book multiple times, whereas I was new to the horrors within its pages.

"Finally," Aunt Zoe continued, "as the *lidérc* gains strength from its host over time, it spreads a pestilence of havoc throughout its immediate surroundings."

"What's 'pestilence' mean, Doc?" Layne asked, checking off something on his paper. "Does that mean lots of bugs start flying around?"

"It's more like a disease," Doc answered, handing me the dice. "It's your turn."

"The great Black Death in the Middle Ages was a pestilence," Cornelius explained, studying his glass of wine. "Interestingly, when the disease initially began to spread, it was actually called 'The Pestilence' or 'The Great Mortality.' Eventually, the 'Black Death' moniker was adopted. This latter namesake was due to the black boils on the bodies that oozed pus and blood."

"Oh, bleck!" I made a retching sound.

"In other words," Aunt Zoe said, looking up from the book at me. "If you were a gladiator hunting a *lidérc*, you would look for surroundings that appear to be diseased. This goes along with how a *lidérc* will gradually kill its host."

"The *lidérc* reminds me of a tarantula hawk wasp," Layne said. "It's parasitic, too. It'll sting a tarantula, putting it into a coma, and then lay its egg on the spider so the larva can slowly eat the tarantula alive after it hatches."

I grimaced, beginning to really not like the word "parasitic." "Did you learn about that in school?"

"No, it was on a show Aunt Zoe and I watched about how insects rule the Earth."

"So, we need to look for someone sickly," Reid said, then glanced at Layne with a wince. "I mean, if we were like one of the gladiators in the book. And all female."

Aunt Zoe stared at him over her reading glasses. "Smooth, Martin."

Look for someone sickly? Being that we were in the middle of the Black Hills snowy season where everyone tended to hole up in their houses until the spring meltoff, we'd have to go door to door. Or we could hang out at the hospital emergency room and watch for eyes that looked like dark mine shafts.

"According to the book on myths I read at the library," Layne said, "a *lidérc* haunts cemeteries at night, too."

I shot Aunt Zoe a frown and moved my token through the secret underground tunnel to the opposite corner, aka the haunted prison.

I looked at the image on the game board of the cemetery, remembering a night under the stars with a sharp-toothed bone cruncher who'd wanted to rip out my throat for fun. I wasn't sure my heart could handle hanging out at a cemetery again in the dark, waiting for a smoky devil that dripped flames. That was right up there with visiting a morgue at night, which I'd done more times than any sane person should while looking for clues about cryptic shipments and mysterious deaths.

"Mom?" Layne moved my token into the haunted prison. "What's your guess?"

Looking for clues …

"Hold on a second, sweetie." I turned to my aunt. "In the book when the other twin sought out the *lidérc* for revenge, does it mention if she used the same clues as her sister to find the *lidérc*?"

"Let me see." She flipped the page, scanning with her finger leading the way. Her lips moved as she read to herself.

While we waited for her to answer my question, I looked at my scrap sheet. "I'm guessing Winchester Wendy caught the ghost in the haunted prison using the audio recorder."

Reid was able to prove me wrong with his Winchester Wendy card.

Aunt Zoe frowned up from the page. "I have good news and bad news. Which do you want to hear first?"

"Wait." I stole a cookie off Cornelius's plate, shoving the whole thing in my mouth. Molasses would help sweeten whatever bad news I was going to have to swallow. "Bad," I mumbled through a mouthful of crumbs.

"There's nothing here about what the gladiator used to find the *lidérc*."

"That's not so bad," I said while covering my mouth so I didn't spit crumbs. It wasn't so good either, since it didn't help me with my *lidérc* hunt.

"I haven't finished. This bit here on the page goes into detail about how the *lidérc* killed the two gladiators."

Doc palmed my thigh, warming it. "I didn't read this part."

She gave me a worried look before proceeding. "When

the *lidérc* attached to the first twin, she burned alive from the inside out. Her skin turned black and blistered within an hour. She was dead by that evening."

"Like the Black Death," Layne said, slurping the last of his soda pop from the bottom of his glass.

"What about the other twin?" Reid asked.

The lines in Aunt Zoe's brow deepened, spreading down her cheeks. "First, she stabbed her own eyes out, then she tried to claw the skin off her face."

"Oh my God," I whispered.

She kept going. "Then she rammed her head into a stone wall over and over until she collapsed." She looked at me over her glasses. "Dead."

I reached for my drink, taking several swallows until Doc pulled it away and placed it back on the table in front of me.

Aunt Zoe set the book down. "According to the notes, a very short time after the *lidérc* infestation, the second twin began to complain about bugs crawling under her skin. Several hours later, she was dead."

"Why would it affect the gladiators so quickly but take years for a human to be drained of life?" Doc asked.

"From what the *magistra* who wrote this section concluded, there is something about the blood running through gladiators that causes the effects to be magnified."

"Maybe it's a form of protection," Cornelius threw out.

"Protection?" I scowled at him. "I think you've gone over your sugar limit tonight." I reached across Aunt Zoe for the last two lemon bars on his plate.

He blocked my hand and held his plate out of my reach. "You're not looking at this from the other side, doppelganger. The *lidérc* isn't able to latch on and gain in strength due to the instant death of the gladiator."

I scoffed at *that* being a form of protection. Seemed too little too late, in my opinion.

"He has a point," Doc said, drawing my frown. "If gladiators are more powerful than humans, then allowing a *lidérc* to attach and gain strength from them is much more dangerous. It's better that the host dies quickly, which forces the *lidérc* to move on to someone else."

"It makes more sense now why the other gladiator Layne told us about jumped off that cliff," Reid said.

Fudge. The results were in: The *lidércs* had three points and the gladiators were still sitting at a big fat zero.

"What's the good news?" I asked my aunt.

"After the gladiator died, the *magistra* was able to protect the children and herself from *lidérc* attachment by coating all in the room with the gladiator's blood."

I gaped at her. "How in the hell is that good news?"

"Mom!" Layne leaned over to Doc and whispered loudly, "She's supposed to say 'heck' in front of company."

"Give her some leeway," Doc said. "She hasn't read the book like we have."

"It's good news," Aunt Zoe explained, "because the gladiator's children were saved and the bloodline was able to go on. Plus, the *magistra* found a protection that could be used. Armor, if you will."

I still gaped. "The armor being the blood of a dead gladiator?"

"Exactly."

I imagined Layne and Addy covered in my blood. The picture in my mind inspired a big chug of my Salty Chihuahua, finishing it off.

I handed Doc my empty glass, needing more tequila. "What's the shelf life of donor blood?"

"Six weeks if stored between one and six degrees Celsius," Cornelius answered without hesitation.

Of course he'd know that. "Did you just pull that out of your ass, Tedious Boris?"

"It's common knowledge."

Maybe for vampires.

"You can store it up to ten years if it's in a freezer at negative sixty-five degrees Celsius," he added, rising from his chair with his empty wine glass.

"No shit." I looked at Reid. "Do you happen to know how to draw blood, Fire Captain Martin?"

"Violet," Aunt Zoe said. "The gladiator was already dead when the *magistra* used her blood for protection."

"And the contamination had already occurred," Doc added, rubbing his fingers over his beard scruff. "There must have been some chemical changes to the gladiator's blood after the infestation."

"In other words," I said to the table at large, "the only way for blood to be used as a barrier is by allowing the *lidérc* to infect the gladiator first, which will be followed almost immediately by her extremely painful death."

"Bingo!" Layne pointed at my hand palming the dice. "Mom, it's Aunt Zoe's turn."

"Talk about a raw deal," I muttered, dropping the dice onto the table in front of her. "Tell me something. Are there any happy endings in that damned book?"

Chapter Six

I once read an article in some psychology magazine about happy endings. In it, the author explained that the emotions a person felt at the end of an event or experience had far more influence in the long term than the crap they went through in the process of reaching the end. In other words, people tended to be willing to rush hell with a bucket of water if there was a happy ending waiting for them.

When I'd read this article, I'd applied it to nine uncomfortable months of pregnancy carrying twins followed by their doubly painful exit from my uterus. After the "crowning" moment following months of aches and hours of labor, I'd held my two happy endings in my arms and cried with joy. But that wasn't really The End on that score.

Now, as I stood in front of the mirror in the upstairs bathroom indulging in my anxiety and premature self-defeat, I tried to apply this happy-ending idea to the task in front of me. Unfortunately, I was having trouble seeing through the dark and terrifying abyss between me and the happily-ever-after rim on the other side.

That was if there was an other side for me.

I puffed my cheeks, letting out a frustrated breath. What was I going to do about that damned *lidérc*?

"I'm fucked," I told the blonde in the mirror with her

straight hair and mascara-smudged eyes.

Aunt Zoe was right—hiding behind a false image wasn't going to cut it. I might appear more sophisticated and in control with straight hair, but underneath my veneer I was still the same old me with quivering legs and trembling hands. Not even tequila could wrangle my mounting stampede of doubts tonight. I could really use my mom's pool of positivity to float in right about now.

I turned my head to the right and then left, trying to look at my profile in the mirror.

Doppelganger, Cornelius had called me.

Was I a harbinger of bad luck? Detective Cooper would agree in a heartbeat, based off the files of unsolved murders stacking up on his desk since I'd arrived in the Black Hills.

I messed up my hair, making it look like I'd scrubbed a balloon on my head. That was more like it. But not quite.

I blew a raspberry at the mirror.

Someone knocked on the bathroom door.

"Yes?" I grabbed the hand towel and tried to wipe away the evidence of my self-pity tears.

"Violet." Doc's voice came through the wood. "It's your turn."

I wet the corner of the towel. I shouldn't have used the cheaper mascara tonight, dang it. "I'll be right there."

"Are you okay?" he asked in a quiet voice after a moment.

"We don't know," the static-haired woman in the mirror answered before I could.

I stuck out my tongue at her and tried to clean off a particularly stubborn smudge in the crease of my left eye.

" 'We'?" Doc tried the locked knob. "Let me in, Killer."

I hesitated, not sure I wanted him to see me in the midst of my wallowing.

"What's the password?" I tried to joke, but my voice cracked on the last syllable.

A pause came from the other side of the door. Then he said quietly, "I've been yours since that first day you carved my initials in your leg."

Gomez Addams! Oh, Doc. He knew exactly what to say.

I rushed over and unlocked the door, opening it wide. "That's my line, *mon cher*."

He stood resting his shoulder against the doorjamb. "Ah, Tish." He cupped my chin, his thumb brushing my cheek as his dark gaze scoured my face. "That's French."

I caught his wrist and pulled him into the bathroom, closing and locking the door behind us.

Doc moved over to the sink vanity, half-sitting on it, one socked foot dangling. "Tell me."

I leaned back, letting the door hold me up. "I don't know if I can handle this Executioner gig."

"The fate of your ancestors won't necessarily be yours."

"But it might be."

He crossed his arms. "If you start focusing on what *could* happen when it comes to the paranormal world, you'll never leave the house again. Trust me, I speak from experience."

"That's not a bad idea."

"What?"

"You and I could hole up together with my kids and Aunt Zoe. We could pay Harvey to deliver food to us and have Cooper monitor our perimeter."

"Violet."

"You were homeschooled, right? Look how well you turned out. We could teach the kids via online courses and spend the rest of our days and nights safe and sound."

He crooked his finger. "Come here."

When I joined him, he took me by the shoulders and turned me to face the mirror, standing behind me. "What do you see?"

"A raccoon-eyed broad with straight hair who ate off

her lip gloss somewhere between the third and fourth molasses cookie."

The corners of his eyes creased. "Nope. Look closer."

I leaned closer to the mirror, noticing some glaze on my cheek and a cookie crumb on my collarbone that I hadn't noticed when I was too busy pity-partying. "A sugar-coated Executioner who bit off more than she can chew."

He slid his hands down my arms, calming me with his touch. "Wrong again, Tish. Try harder."

I sighed, sobering, taking a long hard look at myself. "A mother who is scared shitless that she might have to coat her children in her own blood postmortem in order to keep them alive and safe."

His face lined. "That was a grisly ending for all."

"That seems to be the story of my life these days."

"Not if I can help it." Doc kissed my temple, his beard stubble tickling my cheek. His arms slid around me from behind, pulling me closer. His body heat melted my chills. "You're still not seeing what I am."

"What do you see?" I asked, sinking into him, dropping anchor in the safe harbor he was offering. "Besides the chocolate stain on my shirt?"

His gaze dipped to the stain above my left boob. "Where did that come from? We don't have anything with chocolate downstairs tonight."

"I snuck a truffle the last time I wore this pajama shirt." I rested my head back against his shoulder. "What do you see when you look in the mirror, Oracle?"

"I see a deadly duo who will work together to catch this *lidérc* while keeping you alive and kicking in those sexy purple boots of yours."

I lowered my gaze to my fingers, which were gripping his arms holding me tight. "Doc, I can't let you near that Hungarian bastard." I couldn't lose him. "Nor any of the rest of our posse of misfits."

"I'm not sure you have a choice in the matter, Killer."

I turned to face him. "Doc—"

He placed his index finger over my lips. "Hear me out."

I kissed his finger and then pulled it away. "Okay, but this is my deal with Dominick. I didn't ask any of you for your opinions before offering to catch the *lidérc*, so no one should be responsible for fulfilling the deal but me."

"While that may be true initially, Dominick has altered the deal. This is no longer about a show of power between you two, it's about keeping Zoe out of his slick grip."

I leaned my forehead on his chest, staring down at my abominable snowman slippers. "If something happens to any one of you, I'll never be able to live with myself. I'd sooner follow in the shoes of the Executioner who jumped off the cliff." Better her way of death than the twins', that was for sure.

Doc stroked my hair. "To live without you, *cara mia*, only that would be torture," he said in his Gomez accent.

I smiled up at him in spite of the shitstorm surrounding us. "What are we going to do, *mon cher*?"

"Catch this son of a bitch together." He shifted so he could sit on the sink vanity, settling me between his legs. "Stick with me, *Scharfrichter*, and I'll keep the boogeyman away."

"Tall Medium." I palmed the sides of his face. His beard stubble tickled my fingers. "I love you."

He grinned. "You're just saying that because I brought you a box of cheese."

"Maybe. Maybe so," I said, stealing a line from *Two Mules for Sister Sara.* I brushed my lips over his, tasting the Salty Chihuahua and something sweet. "Or maybe it's because you look super sexy in those candy cane pajama pants. Are you wearing any underwear tonight?" I teased.

He grabbed me by the hips and drew me closer. "Treat me right and I *might* give you a sneak peek later."

I kissed him again, tasting tequila and lemon this time. Hubba hubba. "Is it hot in here or is it just you?"

His chuckle rumbled up from deep in his chest. "All of the static electricity in your hair is heating us up."

"Oh, I don't think my hair is to blame this time." I ran my hands over his shoulders, enjoying the contours. "How about you kiss me good and proper and make me forget about that Hungarian devil for a while?"

" 'Good and proper' isn't going to cut it, Boots." He lowered his mouth toward mine, his hands slipping under my T-shirt. "Not with what I have planned for your lips."

Before we could make contact, someone knocked on the door and then tried to open it.

Thankfully, I'd locked it.

"Mom?" Layne called. "Are you in there?"

Funky monkey! I sighed and pulled away from Doc. "Yes, sweetie."

"It's your turn to roll the dice."

"I told you so," Doc whispered.

"Okay, I'll be down in a minute."

Layne cleared his throat. "Is Doc in there with you?"

I hesitated. I didn't like lying to my kids, but how did I explain Doc being in the bathroom with me?

Doc set me aside and walked over to the door.

What are you doing?!! I mouthed.

He shrugged, unlocked the door, and pulled it open. "Hey, Layne."

Layne took a step back, his gaze narrowing as he looked from Doc to me. "Why is your hair so messy, Mom?"

Ironically, that had nothing to do with the man I was trying to make out with in the bathroom.

"Your mom doesn't like her straight hair," Doc explained.

"I don't really either," Layne said.

"Why not?" I asked, trying to comb through the mess

I'd made of my hair.

"Because you're supposed to have curly hair," he said as if it were clear and simple. "With your hair like that, you sorta look like Aunt Susan."

I flinched. *No!* I looked into the mirror. My God, he was right. I could always trust my children to tell me the painful, humbling truth.

"Ack!" I messed up my hair even more, almost reaching rat's-nest level. "Maybe I should take a quick shower."

Doc laughed. "There's no time for that. We're all waiting for you to come down and take your turn."

"Come on, Mom. Nobody cares about your hair."

"He's right." Doc squeezed Layne's shoulder. "Do me a favor, Dr. Jones, and go see if you can find some ZZ Top in Zoe's music collection."

"On it!" Layne shot me one last worried frown. "Mom, you have something black under your eyes," he said and took off.

" 'Dr. Jones'?" I grabbed the towel and tried to fix my eyes, using a little soap this time.

"As in Dr. Indiana Jones, his hero."

"Oh! Of course." Archaeologist and adventurer extraordinaire, right up Layne's alley.

Doc stood in the doorway, watching me wipe away the smudges. "You look good, Killer. Let's go down and swallow some more tequila."

Nodding, I tossed the towel aside.

"There's a story from your family book that you need to hear," he said as I took his hand.

I hesitated. "Please tell me it's not about an Executioner being chopped into pieces and fed to a great white shark."

He tweaked my chin. "I think you'll like this one."

"Hold that thought." I rushed back to the vanity and grabbed a daisy-covered headband from the drawer, slipping it on. There. Now I looked less like Susan and more like my hippie mom. "That's better." I took his hand again.

He smiled at the headband. "You remind me of your mom now."

"Is that a bad thing?"

"I like your mom. She's funny."

"Good, because she's over the moon about you for being her daughter's white knight."

Like mother, like daughter. Although, truth be told, Doc was more like a dark mysterious knight who could dally with the dead. Hold on … that didn't come out right.

He led me down the hall toward the stairs. "She has that backward. You rescued a lonely old bachelor from a dreary life full of ghosts and ghouls."

More like ghosts and *girls* with Doc's good looks.

"Just wait until I'm finished with you, old bachelor. You'll rue the day you first kissed me in that dark stairwell."

"Not true, *querida*." Gomez was back. "You are the only cactus in the garden of my life."

ZZ Top's guitar riffs kicked to life down in the living room. "La Grange" was blasting from the speakers.

Down in the kitchen, Aunt Zoe greeted me with a worried brow.

I kissed her cheek before taking up the dice. "Let's catch a ghost," I said and rolled.

Chapter Seven

Do the gladiators ever win in that book?" I asked as I moved my token a whopping three spaces on the board.

Doc collected the dice and handed them across to Aunt Zoe. "It's not all doom and gloom while battling demons, devils, and sharp-toothed beasts on the pages."

I pshawed. "Could've fooled me."

"He's right." Layne watched Aunt Zoe roll the dice and move her token out of the haunted hotel where she'd guessed and been proven wrong while I was upstairs. She counted spaces toward the creepy, rundown school, not quite making it inside. "Aunt Zoe, tell Mom the story about the gladiator who teamed up with another from the north to conquer some *navia*."

"What are *navia*?" I took a sip of my drink. Doc had refilled it upon returning from talking me through my bathroom panic attack. "Are they happy-go-lucky spirits who grant wishes and hand out Hawaiian leis when they show up to a party?"

Aunt Zoe chuckled. "Not quite. *Navia* is a generic name in early Slavic mythology for demons that are born from the souls of those who died prematurely or tragically, typically females."

"When you say 'prematurely,' do you mean they were children?"

Her face tightened on one side. "More like young, pretty girls. But the myths vary and also include sorcerers, drowning victims, murderers and their victims. Like I said, it covers a broad range." She pushed the dice toward Cornelius, who was flipping through pages of our family book while tugging on his goatee.

"So what are these *navia* girls like, Zo?" Reid stood over at the counter, munching on crackers and cheese.

"Hostile, jealous of the living, mostly unhappy and not afraid to show it in one way or another."

Reid and I shared smirks. "Sounds like a fun group of demons to have over for a slumber party," I said. "What do they do to the living?"

"Some are believed to be bloodsuckers," Doc answered. "Others cause plagues and spread disease."

"It shows a bird here on the page," Cornelius said, pointing at a drawing in the book. "A blend of a demon with a sharp-clawed raptor would be my guess."

Aunt Zoe leaned over and peered at the book. "I believe the southern Slavs speak of them being in bird form."

Doc's arm slid along the back of my chair, his fingers resting on my shoulder. "I've also read about them appearing in the form of beautiful dancing maidens who lure men to their deaths."

"Dancing maidens are always a nice vision." Reid lifted his glass of whiskey, grinning at Aunt Zoe over the rim. "Remember that night you danced for me under the full moon, Zo?"

She threw a cookie at him, missing her mark only because he dodged it. "Stuff that in your bucket mouth, Martin."

He laughed, picking up the broken cookie pieces from the counter behind him.

"Do they wear belly dancer outfits or frilly tutus?" I

joked, nibbling on another slice of cheese—a nutty Swiss this time.

Doc's gaze dipped below my chin. "A man destined for death can hope for one of those jingling coin, velvet bras."

"It says here they are often half-naked," Cornelius read.

"That'll work, too," Doc said, laughing under his breath when I poked his leg.

"Which half?" Reid asked. "Top or bottom?"

"If they're pretty maidens, does it matter?" Cornelius joined in the fun without looking up from the page.

"They remind me of mermaids," Layne said. "It's your turn, Cornelius."

He looked up from the book, grabbed the dice, and tossed them on the board. "Layne, will you move me into the haunted cemetery."

"Are you sure you want to go in there with all of those chatty ghosts?" I teased the ghost whisperer. His ability to lure the dead, pied piper style, had given both him and Doc problems at séances in the past.

"Definitely." His cornflower blue eyes met mine, a crooked grin on his face. "I've been *dying* to get in there."

Aunt Zoe giggled at his play on words. The whiskey slush must be starting to work its magic on her. "Did you hear about the tornado that tore through a cemetery a few years back?"

"No." Layne frowned at her. "What happened?"

"Hundreds turned up dead." She giggled again.

Doc groaned. "Zoe, that joke was a *grave* mistake."

"Be careful, Doc," Reid said. "You don't want to go getting her stark-*graving* mad. She has a wicked right hook."

I shook my head. "Cornelius, make your guess before I keel over from these ghastly jokes and killer puns."

After a check of his notes, Cornelius made his guess. "Rolling Hills Harry in the haunted cemetery with a 4K HD infrared night vision and full-spectrum hand-held video camera with an IPS screen, 4K UHD wide-angle lens, built-in wi-fi, and an extra battery."

I turned to Doc. "I think that furry hat has possessed him and he's now speaking Russian."

"He means the IR camera."

"I can't help you," Reid said, dropping into his chair.

"Me either." Layne covered a yawn.

Doc slipped Cornelius a card, earning a nod in response. "Thank you, Tall Medium."

"You're welcome, Dr. Zhivago."

Aunt Zoe giggled again and then covered her pink cheeks with her palms. "Uh oh. I should lay off this for a bit." She pushed away her mostly empty glass.

"I disagree, Zo. Your barbs and weapons get softer the more you drink." Reid reached for the dice. "So, what happens in the book to those poor guys chasing after the mermaid gals?"

"*Navia*, Martin." Aunt Zoe pulled her hair over her shoulder and started braiding it. "The details are sparse, but from what I can remember, there were multiple *navia* causing trouble in a western Slav town in what is now Poland. And by *trouble*, I mean gruesome deaths."

I started to ask her to clarify the "gruesome" part, but then I remembered that Layne was participating in this conversation, not to mention that we were supposed to be focusing on happy stories now, so I kept my mouth shut.

"Two gladiators joined up to battle the *navia*," Layne said, his voice high with excitement. "One was a girl in the book and the other came from somewhere in the north, like Russia. They kicked the *navia's* butts."

I doubted it was a simple fight if it took two Executioners to take care of the job. "So the gladiator from the book spoke the other's language?"

"Many of the gladiators in this book are multilingual," Aunt Zoe explained.

That's where I fell short. Aunt Zoe had been taught Latin and German by my great-grandmother, who was supposedly an incredible *magistra* with abilities bordering that of a seer. She lived by her rune stones and scared the crap out of me with her scratchy voice, rattling off eerie prophecies about me having hidden dangers in my pockets. She also was fond of telling me that I smelled of death. I can't remember how many baths I took trying to wash that scent off my skin.

Reid took his turn, moving toward the fire station but falling a few spaces short. "How did they catch these *navia* babes?"

"It says here that they had to do it in the winter when the marsh and lake were frozen over," Cornelius said, poring over the book again.

Aunt Zoe looked at Cornelius. "Isn't there something about a hole being cut into the ice?"

"It was sort of like ice fishing," Doc told Reid.

"What did they use for bait?" I asked, watching Layne roll the dice and follow Reid's lead, heading for the fire station. There must be a party happening there, because Doc was aiming for it, too.

"It talks about the need for a …" Cornelius held out the book to Aunt Zoe. "What's this word?"

"*Der Beschwörer.*"

Cornelius repeated it, not sounding quite as smooth as Aunt Zoe. "But it says none of those were available, so they used human males instead."

"What's *Der Beschwörer*?" I asked.

Aunt Zoe stared down at the end of her braid, her expression sobering. "A Summoner."

There was something about the gravity of her tone that gave me pause. Before I could prod about what was going on in her head, Reid asked Cornelius, "What do you mean, they 'used' human males?"

"If memory serves me right from when I transcribed that part," Aunt Zoe cut in, shooting a sly grin at her old flame, "the gladiators dangled a human male over the hole in the ice to lure the *navia* up from the freezing depths."

"Was the guy dead?" I asked.

"Of course not. The *navia* seek the living, so they can steal their souls. Remember, they're a rather jealous lot, quite unhappy about being dead."

"The gladiators just dangled the poor guy over the hole?" Reid asked, his voice higher with indignation.

"Not quite. They needed blood to catch a *navia*."

"Like chumming for sharks," Layne said and grabbed a handful of mixed nuts from the bowl sitting between him and Reid.

"They'd remove a hand from the ... uh ... *bait*," Aunt Zoe explained. "The fresh blood would continue to drip into the water that way."

The appalled expression on Reid's face would have been comical if I wasn't experiencing some of the same jaw-dropping feelings.

"Holy shhh—" Reid noticed he had Layne's attention mid-curse and left it at that. He aimed a glower at me. "That's just cold-blooded, Sparky."

"What?" I held my hands up in defense. "I didn't do it."

"Yeah, but it reminds me of someone else who likes to use bait to tempt trouble."

I cringed, remembering that night in the Sugarloaf building when I'd dangled Reid out there to hook the *lidérc*.

"Good things come to those who bait," Cornelius said without looking up.

"You're not helping," I told Boris the bonehead.

Aunt Zoe snorted. "And those who play with fire don't like it when they get burned."

I glanced her way, finding her staring daggers at her ex. Was she talking about the *lidérc*, who dripped flaming embers when it was outside of a human host, or a certain fire captain who'd once burned her heart badly and left it covered with scars?

I nudged her glass of whiskey slush even farther away from her. "Let's get back to the story." I leaned on the table, propping up my chin with my hand. "So, the *navia* were lured up through the fishing hole by the guy's blood. Then what?"

"The book says …" Cornelius followed the written text with his finger. "As soon as a demon stuck her head out of the water, one of the gladiators would snare it with a *Mannfänger*."

"What's a *Mannfänger*?" I asked Doc.

Layne beat him to the answer. "It's a long rod with a steel collar on one end that has these sharp spikes on the inside." My son's eyes were all sparkly from either the sugar tonight, the talk of medieval weapons, or both.

"The jaws are pushed around the neck," Doc added, using his hands to demonstrate. "Then they snap shut after the neck passes through. Some cultures have used it as a torture device."

"Jeez," Reid said. "First they dangled a poor sucker over the hole in the middle of winter, cut off his hand, and let him just drip. Then they slapped one of these torture devices on a beautiful young maiden?"

"Beautiful, young, half-naked maiden," Cornelius clarified.

"Sounds like someone besides the *navia* were jealous." Reid smirked at Aunt Zoe. "And these gladiators were supposed to be on the good side?"

Her gaze challenged him. "Catching *navia* was no task for a mere male, Martin."

I rested my hand on her arm in case she decided to throw something else at Reid. "What did they do with the *navia* after they had them locked in those spiky jaws?"

Doc rolled the dice. "While one held the *navia* in the *Mannfänger*," he said, moving his token into the fire station, "the other gladiator clubbed it to death."

I winced at the violent images that spurred in my head. That sounded like my bloodline, all right—we were the juggernauts of the Executioner world. Club-thumping was our specialty.

Reid stared at me like I was the one holding the bloody club. "That's so wrong."

"They were *navia*, Martin," Aunt Zoe defended. "Not baby seals."

"Still," he said, shaking his head.

"Jealous, life-stealing demons," she continued, "that would drag a son of a ... I mean a man ... down to their depths and eat his soul."

'You said steal his soul before." He crossed his arms. "I thought this was supposed to be a happy story."

"It is," she said, patting my hand that was still resting on her arm. "The gladiators worked together to take out a bunch of *navia*. It took them over a month to complete the task, if I remember right."

"There's a tally here," Cornelius flipped the page. "Over thirty-three nights of hunting, they caught and killed twenty-four *navia*, and it took only six human males to complete the task."

"Six?" I tipped my head to the side. There was that number again.

"It was really only four if you read further down," Aunt Zoe told me. "The first two didn't count."

"Why not?"

"Because the first guy slipped out of the rope they were using and fell down through the hole, drowning under the ice before they could fish him back out."

Criminy! That sounded like one of my monumental screwups. "And the second?"

"The gladiators cut off his leg at the knee and he drained out too quickly. After that, they stuck to only taking a hand."

"Lesson learned," I said, sitting back in my chair, looking at my hands. Same as I'd learned that cutting off the arm of certain "others" might not kill them, so sometimes it was more effective to jam a corkscrew bottle opener into their neck until they sort of spontaneously combusted and only ashes were left.

When I looked up, all eyes but Layne's were on me. "What?"

Reid scowled deeper. Cornelius shook his head and returned to the pages of the book. Doc scratched his jaw and traded grins with Aunt Zoe.

"It's your turn to guess, Doc," Layne reminded him.

"I still don't see how any of that was a happy story," Reid said, taking a drink.

"Martin." Aunt Zoe tossed her braid over her shoulder. "Have you considered that maybe the males the gladiators used as bait were known criminals? They could have been plucked from the local jail, guilty of rape or murder or something worse."

"They could have cut off other certain male appendages, too," I added with a smile. "But they didn't."

"The gladiators in those stories had a job to do," Aunt Zoe said to all at the table. "First and foremost, they needed to protect humankind. Sometimes that meant getting their hands dirty in the process."

"Doc?" Layne pressed.

"I'm going for the win, Dr. Jones." He grabbed the cards laying facedown in the Boo-ville town square. "I think it was Alcatraz Al sneaking around in Fire Captain Martin's haunted fire station with the Poltercom."

We all checked our cards while Doc looked at the three cards from the town square. He tossed them on the table with a smile. "Nailed it."

"Ahhh, dang." Reid handed his cards to Layne. "That was going to be my next guess."

"Mine, too," Layne said, collecting the rest of our cards.

"You boys are just too slow," Doc teased, standing to stretch. He headed over to the sink and filled a glass with water.

I watched my son sort and mix the cards as I rubbed my neck. Something that Aunt Zoe had said earlier in the story poked at me. "Aunt Zoe, are there any other stories about … what was it called … *Der Bo* … a Summoner?"

"Why?" she asked.

"I'm curious."

"Is that the only reason?"

"What other reason would I have?"

She shrugged. Something about the way she was studying her fingernails made me frown.

"There is one," Layne spoke up. "But it's gross."

Doc chuckled and lifted the glass to his mouth.

"Why is it gross?" I asked, looking to Aunt Zoe for answers. "What happens to the gladiator in this one?"

"She had babies," Layne said with a good dose of disgust. "Lots of them."

"Were they demon babies?" Reid asked.

"No," Doc said, setting his glass down on the counter. "They were a Summoner's babies. The two of them ended up …" He hesitated, glancing at Layne.

"Mating," Aunt Zoe finished.

"Really?" I said, sitting up in my chair.

Doc returned to the table. "This is the story I mentioned upstairs."

"What time frame in history was this?" Cornelius asked, flipping through several pages.

"The mid-Renaissance," Doc said, grabbing the bowl of nuts I'd filled earlier. "It was a romantic time for all, apparently." He ate a cashew. "Even the gladiators."

"Yuck." Layne moved everyone's tokens back to their respective starting spots. "If you guys are going to tell this story, I'm going to the bathroom."

"Well, you'd better skedaddle, kiddo," Aunt Zoe said. "Because your mom could use a little romance tonight."

It would be a pleasant change from gruesome deaths.

"Isn't romancing Sparky supposed to be Nyce's job?" Reid asked as soon as Layne was out of earshot.

Doc lifted my hand and kissed my knuckles, wiggling his eyebrows at me. "I have the *Mannfänger* tucked away upstairs for later, Tish."

I patted his cheek. "Don't torture yourself, *mon cher*. That's my job." I heard a door slam upstairs and leaned closer to Aunt Zoe. "Does a Summoner mating mean what I think it means?"

"That depends." Aunt Zoe matched my volume.

"On what?"

"On what you think it means."

"We have Summoner genes in our DNA."

"Then, yes, it means what you think it means."

I frowned. "But what does that mean exactly?"

"We're hybrids. I've told you that before."

"But you said we were a human hybrid." At least that's what she'd told me after one of the "others" said I was only part human.

"Well, after these two mated and produced multiple offspring, we became a human–Summoner hybrid, which is very rare."

But was this a good or bad rarity? "So these Summoners don't usually mate with Executioners?"

"No. Summoners are …" She tapped her fingernail on her glass, chewing on her lower lip. "Well, let's just say they're problematic."

"Why's that?" Doc asked.

"For one thing, they're always male." She squinted at Reid. "That in itself can be trouble."

Reid raised his whiskey glass to her. "Trouble is my middle name, sweetheart."

She harrumphed. "The other hitch is that they do as their name describes. They summon."

"Summon what, though?" I asked.

"You name it—devils, demons, deadly beasts, and creatures of all foul realms and planes."

"Sounds like a good-time guy, if you ask me," Reid said.

Cornelius looked up from the book. "Why would they summon? To what end?"

"Well, they don't always do it on purpose. Sometimes they're unaware of their power."

I rubbed the back of my neck, thinking about how summoning could be abused in the wrong hands.

"Often in history," Aunt Zoe continued, "they're killed while young, like Executioners."

"You mean by the creatures they summon?" Doc asked.

"No. It's not easy for an 'other' to kill a Summoner. They heal quickly from even the deepest wounds delivered by these beings. Usually, they're killed by humans."

I did a double-take. "Why?"

"Because they're often labeled as sorcerers or witches or bringers of curses." She stirred her whiskey slush. "When it is speculated that the Summoner is the one attracting the malevolence, humans often try to rid themselves of the problem by killing the Summoner. Unfortunately, this doesn't solve anything and their enemy is now free to terrorize at will."

"That's a horrible thing to be born into," I said.

"Being an Executioner isn't exactly a sought-after role," she said, bumping my hand. "You are hunted as well, only instead of humans coming with torches and pitchforks, you are the prey of a darker, more dangerous legion."

"If you're trying to make me feel better, you're failing miserably."

"What exactly do Summoners do besides draw the worst of the worst out of the woodwork?" Reid asked.

"They lead trouble away from humans, acting as bait. While they don't have the ability to kill things the same way that Executioners do, their blood is poisonous to most other creatures. So, as I said before, they're not easy to kill by non-human hands."

"Let me get this straight." I laced my fingers together. "Summoners are magnets for the shitty creatures out there meant to do harm in the world, but they cannot kill these creatures when they show up on their doorstep."

"Correct."

"But if the creatures take a bite out of them, they are deadly to the attacker?"

"Basically. Often, Summoners are sought by those who want to wreak havoc on humanity. They're used as bait to draw out the wicked from the other realms, as in creatures that will be used to destroy and conquer."

"And one of our ancestors mated with a Summoner?"

"The more romantic version is that they fell in love," Doc said, stealing a cracker from my plate.

"Okay," I told them both. "Let's hear it."

Aunt Zoe took the book from Cornelius and flipped forward several pages. "There was a *gaueko* running free in the Basque region of northern Spain."

"What's a *gaueko*?" Reid scooped up a handful of nuts. "Another pretty maiden out to kill poor, gullible hunters?"

"A spirit of the night," Aunt Zoe said. "Some think of it as a devil. It punishes those who are brave enough to walk through the forest in the dark."

"Punishes them how?" I asked, wincing in anticipation. I doubted it strapped them to the bed and tickled them to death with feathers.

"It guts them and tears off their limbs, leaving them tied upside down in the forest trees."

"A real darling of a devil there," I muttered.

Doc snorted. "It hides in gusts of wind, invisible to the naked eye. Once it sets upon a victim, it swirls around them, confusing the human. Then it appears before them as a beast with red eyes, four horns that look like gnarled tree branches, and thick craggy gray skin."

GAUEKO

Aunt Zoe shifted in her chair. "By that point, there's no running. You're dead meat."

"I thought you said this was a romance," I said to Doc.

"Wait for it."

"The Summoner was living in the Basque region," Aunt Zoe said, glancing down at the book. "According to the brief notes about him, his father had been a Summoner before him from further south in Spain, and his mother was a sorceress of Basque heritage. After his father was murdered—"

"Why was his father murdered?" I interrupted.

"It doesn't say why in the book," Doc answered.

"After his father was murdered," Aunt Zoe continued, "the Summoner's mother fled to her home region in northern Spain and used her sorcery to hide her son's abilities from the humans around them. But as he aged and his powers strengthened, hers weakened. In time, the son's summoning powers came into play and drew the *gaueko* to them. The mother was able to shield her son, but at her own expense. Drained, she was no match for the creature. What the *gaueko* didn't know was that the sorceress had already recruited an Executioner to help her son—our ancestor, Ayla."

"Ayla?" I looked down at the book. "Do they always mention Executioners' names in that book?"

"No, but Ayla was special, and her *magistra* had great pride in her. Plus, she ofen wore a long purple cloak to battle, which your son thinks is very cool. He calls it her superwoman cape."

"Special how?" Cornelius asked. "Did she have medium abilities?"

"She was a strong, well-seasoned Executioner who had made many difficult kills in the Black Forest region. The *magistra* listed her age as near three decades."

Ayla.

I imagined a tall, strong blond woman with sexy abs and killer thighs like the old Barbarella Queen of the Galaxy movie posters, her purple cloak blowing behind her in the wind. "Did the *magistra* list the Summoner's name?"

"'Charan the Basque' is all that's written."

Reid crunched on some more nuts. "So this poor guy, Charan, acted as bait so that Ayla could kill this *Gaueko* creature? I'm detecting a fishing theme here."

Aunt Zoe glared at him over the top of her reading glasses for several seconds. "Anyway, it took them a fortnight for the *gaueko* to return to the forest."

"Why so long if Charan was a Summoner?" I asked.

"The *gaueko* is a cautious foe. Most are very old and extremely wise. After the sun set, Charan was able to draw the *gaueko* out into the open and trick it into taking its four-horned, beast form in front of him. But before it could attack Charan, Ayla stepped in between them and slew it."

Cornelius grunted. "How'd she kill it?"

Reid didn't give Aunt Zoe a chance to answer him. "With what kind of weapon?"

I didn't either. "Was it an easy kill?"

"The book doesn't say," was her response to all of us.

We cursed in unison.

She chuckled. "It only says that she slew the *gaueko* and Charan followed her back to the Black Forest. Once there, they had eight children."

"Eight?" My jaw hit the table. "Sheesh, Charan must have been quite a stud."

"Well, he was Basque," Aunt Zoe said with a wink. "Have you seen some of those guys? Tall, dark, and hewn from stone. Can you blame Ayla?"

"Yeah, but *eight* kids?"

"Interestingly, there were three sets of fraternal twins, and two boys. Our line is quite prone to twins."

Yeah, yeah, yeah, history repeats itself and all of that

jazz. My uterus cringed at the thought of carrying and pushing out three sets of twins.

I sighed, lowering my head onto my arms on the table. "How am I supposed to figure out how to kill some of these damned demons and monsters without more details?"

"I told you before, Violet Lynn, this book is not a how-to-kill guide. It's more of a who-they-were and how-they-died reference. Besides, what worked for Ayla will not necessarily work for you."

Doc rubbed my back as I moped on the table. "The good news, Killer, is that Ayla lived a long life."

"It's amazing those eight kids weren't the death of her," I said, looking up at my aunt.

She handed the book back to Cornelius. "Ayla is one of the few in our line to live to old age, so it can be done."

"Eight kids would turn me into a mad hatter." I was still hung up on all of those babies.

"Ayla saved our line. She was the last Executioner after years of bitter battles in the Black Forest prior to the Renaissance period. Her mother was an Executioner before her, but she was killed by a demon troll."

I sat up. "You're kidding me. Another troll?"

"There's a name for the creature, but it escapes me at the moment."

"How many kinds of trolls are there?" Maybe my kids' sperm donor was part troll.

"Anyway," Aunt Zoe said, patting my forearm. "You asked for a happy story, and now I've given you two."

"I don't know. Eight babies are more of a nightmare."

Reid snorted in agreement. "Using human males as bait isn't exactly the makings of seasons in the sun."

"In your line of work, Violet Lynn, you can't be choosy where you find your happiness. Take your joy where you can, because the road you walk is often dark and full of deadly beings wanting to tear you to pieces."

I scoffed, turning to Doc. "We should make that into an inspirational poster starring Wilda's half-burned clown doll."

Doc shook his head. "You Aries ladies sure know how to make a relationship fun and interesting."

"Aries typically have a high sex drive, too," Cornelius said out of left field, making Reid burst out laughing.

Layne's thumping footfalls coming down the stairs warned us all to switch back to pretending the Executioner business was pure fiction.

He jogged into the kitchen. "What did I miss?" he fell into his chair and looked at Aunt Zoe. "Did you tell her about all of the babies?"

"She did," Doc said, laughing at the pained expression Layne made. "It made your mom squirm, too."

"Don't worry, kiddo," Aunt Zoe said. "The next story I'm going to tell your mom is one of your favorites."

Layne rubbed his hands together. "Is it the one about the Romanian castle imp or that creepy monster that slithers and melts into the shadows?"

My vote was for an imp. In movies, they were usually small with less sharp teeth, more mischievous than threatening.

"It's the tale about the *Nalusa Falaya*."

I frowned back and forth between her and Layne. "The what?"

"Oh, good," he said, dealing out the cards. "I like how that gladiator learns how to see while she's in the dark."

Chapter Eight

I'd always sucked at being a loner.

Maybe it came from being a middle child, or maybe it was just the way I was wired, but for as long as I could remember I'd always had someone at my side.

First there was my three-years-older brother. My parents had put my crib in Quint's room, forcing him to bunk with me from the get-go. By the time I was old enough to move out of his bedroom, Susan had come along and needed a room to share, and mine was it. She'd been my shadow as soon as she could crawl, always there next to me watching while I played with my toys. After her watching turned into breaking and our tiffs grew into all-out brawls, my parents moved Quint into the basement, gave Susan his room, and kept us all separated for their sanity probably more than ours.

But I wasn't alone even then because by that time I'd found Natalie, who became my best friend within ten minutes of meeting her. She was a fixer and some part of me was always broken, so we shared a symbiotic relationship based on mutual benefit. Although there were times when I felt more tick-like, such as after I'd found out I was pregnant with twins with no financial help in sight. The only way she could "fix" me then was to help hold me up until I could find my feet again.

My parents had always been by my side, taking me in

time and again so that I didn't have to stand alone. Of course, after Addy and Layne joined me in this world, I was rarely if ever on my own. While I may have accidentally signed up for this parenting gig, I'd taken my single mother role seriously and left my kids only for work and an occasional decompressing night out with Natalie.

And then there was Aunt Zoe, who'd opened her home to us this last year and rescued me from my parents' basement. Now Doc was in my life day and night, too. Not to mention Harvey, Cornelius, Reid, my coworkers—hell, even Cooper.

What was my point …

Oh, yeah, I was not much of a loner, but I had a very dangerous devil to catch. A human parasite, and death was the only known means of extraction.

And Executioners usually worked alone.

Did I take a page from Ayla and the *navia* slayers and hunt this *lidérc* with some help, risking the loss of someone I loved to its life-sucking embrace?

Or did I hunt the Hungarian bastard on my own? After all, I had an advantage over my enemies now thanks to Ms. Wolff passing her "timekeeper" torch to me before she'd died. Actually, she'd passed her clock-monitoring ability to me after telling me that my skills as a *Scharfrichter* would not be enough to keep me alive for long, and that becoming a timekeeper would build my strength in a way that my enemies would not expect.

But I was still learning how to make this timekeeper gig work in my favor.

It would be so easy to let Doc and Natalie and all of the others help me. But they were not fellow killers, like my *navia*-fishing ancestor and the Russian Executioner, nor did they carry Summoner blood in their veins to protect them, as was the case of Charan. Was I willing to take the risk of including them in this game of hide and seek with the *lidérc* so I wouldn't have to be alone?

"Mom!" Layne's voice cut through my dilemma woes. "It's your turn."

I blinked away my worries, hiding behind a quick smile, and picked up the dice someone had set in front of me. I rolled a pair of threes—six.

What was with that number tonight? Maybe I should buy a lottery ticket with all sixes on it. Or buy six lottery tickets.

I moved my token six places, aiming for the haunted hospital. "So, what's a *Nalufa Salala?*"

"*Nalusa Falaya,*" Aunt Zoe corrected. "It's from the Choctaw tribe's mythology."

Cornelius looked up from the book, one eyebrow raised almost high enough to hide under his Cossack hat. "You mean the Choctaw tribe that was originally in the southeastern United States?"

"That's them." Aunt Zoe took the dice I held out.

"My grandmother from Louisiana had many tales about the Choctaw and their myths of old."

"What kind of tales?" Reid asked, watching Aunt Zoe roll the dice.

"The kind that will raise the hair on the back of your neck."

I stifled a moan. At this rate I was going to have a thick coat of hair running down my back by midnight.

After Aunt Zoe moved a few spaces out of her starting spot, I tapped her arm. "Let's hear the story about this *Nalusa Fa-la-la.*"

"*Falaya.*" She enunciated each syllable this time. "Don't worry, this one doesn't end with a gladiator dying."

"Yeah, but—" my son started.

"Layne," Aunt Zoe interrupted, holding her index finger to her lips. "Let me tell the tale to your mother."

Reid pushed back his chair and walked over to the

fridge. "What time period are we talking for this story, Zo?"

"Late 1600s."

"The Renaissance was over," Doc added.

Reid grabbed a jar of strawberry jam and carried it to the counter. "So, this story takes place after Ayla and Charan's story and involves their offspring?"

"Right." She frowned as he grabbed a knife from the drawer. "What are you doing?"

"Adding a strawberry topping to your lemon bars." He motioned for her to keep going. "Sparky is waiting to hear your story."

With her brow wrinkled, Aunt Zoe turned back to the table and nudged the dice toward Cornelius. "This particular gladiator came over to the New World with some French traders—one of whom was her husband. Life had quieted down over in the Black Forest region when it came to killing, as things tend to do for generations at a time until the need for gladiators is set in motion again." She looked pointedly at me.

As life had quieted down for multiple generations before me—I got it.

"But they didn't have any babies yet," Layne added, his upper lip wrinkled at the mere thought of offspring.

I got that, too. The idea of more babies gave me the hives. I'd sooner face off with a *lidérc* in the dark.

"Soon after arriving in what is now the Louisiana area," Aunt Zoe said, "she befriended some women from the local Choctaw tribe and began to learn their language. That winter, two things happened: The gladiator got pregnant—" Layne and I both cringed visibly, making Aunt Zoe chuckle before she continued. "The other thing was that she began to hear news about a shadow in the forest that was preying on the Choctaw—hunters, women, and children alike. Basically, anyone who strayed too deep into the forest alone."

Reid set down a plate with three lemon bars covered with strawberry jam on the table in front of his chair. "This shadow was the *Nalusa Falaya*, I take it."

She nodded, scowling at the bars. "They were perfectly fine without that."

"They were delicious without it, but now they're downright mouth-watering. Remember all the fun things we used to do with your sweet and sticky strawberry jam, Zo?" He took a big bite of a bar, smiling wide behind closed lips as he chewed.

Her cheeks took on a color similar to the strawberry jam. She glared at him for a couple of heartbeats before turning back to me. "Anyway, the gladiator snuck out several nights in a row with her mace, hunting the elusive shadow demon, but she was unable to lure it out."

Cornelius rolled snake eyes, moving his token two spaces before pushing the dice toward Reid. His hand paused near Reid's plate with the two remaining strawberry-covered lemon bars.

"Take one," Reid said around a bite and tossed the dice. "Everything's better with strawberry jam on it."

"Tell her about the Choctaw seer," Layne urged as Reid moved five spaces up Boo-ville's Skeleton Street.

"I'm getting there, kiddo." She watched Cornelius take a bite, glowering as he nodded at Reid and stuck the rest of the strawberry lemon bar in his mouth.

Huffing, she focused back on me. "A short time later, the gladiator's husband left for several days to trek inland and trade with other tribes. The next morning, she found out the daughter of one of her Choctaw friends had gone missing. The gladiator went to the tribal elders straight away and told them she wanted to hunt the shadow that they called *Nalusa Falaya* come nightfall. She needed their permission in case she had to trek across sacred lands in the process. The elders were against the idea. Not only was she a female, but they also knew about her being with child. Unfortunately, that night one of their best hunters was slain."

"All they found was his head," Layne added in a spooky voice, his face alight with excitement.

"Seriously," I told him. "You need to lay off the history books about weapons, myths, and monsters. They're warping your brain."

Doc laughed, fist-bumping Layne.

"The next afternoon, the tribe's leaders sent for the gladiator," Aunt Zoe said, watching Layne move his token toward the haunted fire station. "When she arrived, they took her deep into the forest, leaving her in a shelter made of animal skins with a blind man from their tribe."

Reid wiped his hands on his napkin. "They left her with a blind guy?"

"He was blind," Doc explained. "But he was a seer."

"Interesting," Cornelius said, steepling his fingers.

Reid scoffed. "Let me guess, the poor blind guy is going to be used as bait."

Aunt Zoe reached across the table and stole the last strawberry-covered lemon bar from Reid's plate.

"Hey!" He pretended to be offended, ruining it with a flirty smile as he watched her take a bite and lick her lips.

"The seer spent several hours with the gladiator," she resumed the story, "chanting while various herbs and leaves simmered in a pot over a nearby fire. When he finished, it was dark outside. He brought the pot over to her and instructed her to close her eyes, breathe in the steam, and picture the *Nalusa Falaya* standing in front of her."

That reminded me of Cornelius sitting up at Mount Moriah Cemetery next to Wild Bill's grave, teaching me how to see in the dark. Only he had me close my eyes and picture a candle flame, forgetting to mention at the time that I wasn't supposed to reach out with my mind because there were things in the dark waiting to kill me.

"According to the story, the gladiator believed she fell asleep while her eyes were closed only to wake up a short time later to the sound of someone screaming. However, when she opened her eyes, there was no screaming, only gargled sounds coming from the blind man who was being strangled by a dark shadowy figure with yellow eyes.

The gladiator grabbed her mace and fought the *Nalusa Falaya*, sending it back to the hell whence it had come."

"Don't you mean, 'from whence,' Zo?" Reid watched Aunt Zoe lick the strawberry jam from her fingers with rapt attention.

"Whence means 'from where,' Martin." She gave him a hard look. "Stick to playing with fire, hose jockey, and leave working with language to me."

"I am," he said, reaching for his drink.

"So, the gladiator lured it to her by going into the dark," Cornelius said, repeating what I'd thought as well.

Doc plucked up the dice. "Maybe she was an ectoplasmic medium and was able to bring the *Nalusa Falaya* back from another plane."

"Ectoplasmic medium" was what Cornelius had called me after the séance we'd had in Harvey's barn a couple of months ago. Apparently, it meant I could locate a creature in another realm or plane or whatever and then wake up to find it hanging out with me in my regular world. Cornelius found this ability awe-striking. I found it utterly terrifying and worried about falling asleep because of it many a night since.

Doc glanced at me before tossing the dice on the board. "Reminds me of another story I've heard."

I grimaced and chanced a look at Layne, but he was too busy eating colored popcorn off a garland string to notice the undercurrent at the table right then.

"Did anything bad happen to the gladiator?" I asked Aunt Zoe, who'd moved to the sink to wash her hands. "Or her baby?"

"Nothing is mentioned, although the Choctaw elders kept secret what had happened. They told the rest of the tribe that a ceremony had been performed to send away the evil spirit and that was it."

"They probably wanted to protect her reputation," Doc

said. "A foreigner with what some might believe are sorceress abilities could be deemed malevolent by some."

Right, the same bad rap that Summoners received. "What was the baby's gender when it was born?"

"There were two—a boy and a girl."

"Ugh, more twins."

Doc moved his token into the haunted police station. "Zoe, is it just me or were the twins always fraternal in those stories after Ayla and Charan got together?"

Aunt Zoe nodded, drying her hands on a dish towel. "Other aspects of the stories after their mating certainly shifted as well."

"Shifted how?" I asked.

"There were fewer deaths from then on. My theory is that Charan's Summoner and sorcery lineage caused a beneficial genetic change that increased the gladiators' success rate."

"But were there fewer who died due to this shift or were there fewer needs for a gladiator?" Doc asked. "After all, if you look at history, the Dark Ages were over by the time they met. While there were still wars and battles, the violence had abated ... at least for a while."

Aunt Zoe shrugged. "The writings in the book don't contain an answer to that question."

"Are there other more recent stories in there?" I pointed at the book.

"There are a few tales here and there, but much of what's left is for the *magistrae*."

For her kind, not mine, in other words. "Like what?"

She draped the towel over the faucet. "Instructions, poultice recipes, lineage details."

"It gets boring at the end," Layne said, rubbing his eyes. "Full of all kinds of symbols and words written in some weird language."

Aunt Zoe smiled at him as she returned to the table.

"That's Latin, honey. Maybe I'll teach you someday if you're interested."

"Would you really?"

"Sure. Should we teach Addy, too?"

He yawned. "Nah, she doesn't like to read like me."

"Neither does her mother," Aunt Zoe said, chuckling when I wrinkled my nose at her. "Will you do me a favor, Layne, and run up to my bedroom closet and grab the black box in the back corner?"

"Sure, but it's Doc's turn to guess, so somebody needs to tell me what he says."

"We will," I told him. As soon as Layne was out of earshot, I whispered to her, "Are we direct descendants of the Executioner who helped the Choctaw?"

"No. She would be your ..." she counted on her fingers for a moment. "Well, she'd be a great times-too-many-to-count aunt. Her and her children were killed several years later when they returned to Germany after her husband died. She told this *Nalusa Falaya* story to her grandmother upon returning, who was the acting *magistra* at that time. We are actually descendants of that Executioner's brother. He had five children—all boys but one, your ancestor."

"No twins?" Doc asked.

"Interestingly, only the females in our line have twins. The males, like Violet's father, breed only one child at a time." She leaned forward. "Even more curious, after studying the family tree I noticed something else—twins usually come only when there is a need for an Executioner. It's as if creating children in twos ensures the chances of the family line's continuation."

In other words, my twins were not a happy accident. What did that mean for their futures? For mine?

"Tell me, Violet's Aunt, when did your family emigrate from Germany?" Cornelius's fingers returned to their steepled position.

"In the early 1800s. They didn't make their way west until my grandmother moved here a century ago."

"Do you think she knew there was trouble coming?" Doc asked. He tugged on a lock of my hair. "Besides Killer here, I mean."

I pretended to try to bite his finger.

"It's possible," Aunt Zoe said, looking at me. "She did use her rune stones daily."

I shuddered, remembering the sound of those clacking rune stones all too well.

"It's also possible that she was drawn here because the Black Hills are a lot like Germany's Black Forest."

"Your family moved from one hotspot to another," Reid said.

"Perhaps." She looked at me with a worried brow. "Although there have been no twins born for a very long time until Violet's."

The creak of the stair steps quieted us.

Layne came into the kitchen carrying a dusty, black wooden box with some elaborate scrolls on the sides. His load wasn't light, judging from his struggles to lift it onto the table.

"What's that?" I asked.

She took the box from him and lifted the lid. "More family history."

I blinked, soaking up what she'd said. Then I blinked again. "More?"

"I told you months ago, Violet, that there were several volumes." She lifted out three more books, stacking them on the table between us.

I shot Doc a holy-shit look. He frowned back at me.

"Oh, man!" Layne bounced up and down next to her chair. "Can I read them?"

"These are written in Old German and Latin. I haven't had a chance to transcribe what's on the pages, so you'll have to do some learning before you can help me decipher the stories."

"Uh, Aunt Zoe." I leaned away from the books, afraid of what was inside of them, and bumped into Doc. "What's in those?" I hoped like hell it was a bunch of boring ramblings about favorite foods and weather anomalies.

"In these?" She wiped the dust off the one on top. "Just a few more gladiator stories from the Dark Ages."

Chapter Nine

And then the sky fell.

At least that was what it felt like in my head—minus the chicken running around squawking about it. Maybe I should bring Elvis up from the basement and let 'er run.

I frowned at the three books. That didn't look like just a *few* more stories to me.

My chest grew tight, my breath coming faster.

Jeez and crackers! I'd set out tonight to figure out how to snare a *lidérc* only to realize that catching the damned Hungarian devil might be the least of my problems.

Three books!

Sweet Jesus, the odds of seeing my children into adulthood were now a long shot at best.

It was hard to swallow around the egg-sized lump of panic in my throat. I had to vent for a minute or I was going to go into cardiac arrest.

"Layne, plug your ears," I ordered.

"Why?"

"Because I'm going to use words I'd rather you didn't hear me say."

Layne's face screwed up in a perplexed expression. "But I've heard you cuss a lot of times before, Mom."

"Plug your ears anyway. And close your eyes, too." I didn't trust him not to read my lips.

He sighed, putting his index fingers in his ears. "Okay,

but just so you know I can still hear you when you yell."

After he'd squeezed his eyelids shut, I turned to Aunt Zoe, talking low. "You mean to tell me that this other fucking book we've been talking about tonight contains shit that happened only *after* the Dark Ages?"

She nodded.

"And those three damned books contain stories from a single fucking period of time?"

"Well, it was about one thousand years, give or take a century."

"One thousand years of hellish encounters?!" My voice rose at the end.

"I heard that, Mom," Layne said almost as loud as me, his eyes still closed tight.

"Yes, Violet." She pointed at the book on the bottom of the stack. "But this first book here also covers some of the time prior to the Dark Ages. I've only skimmed them, though, but the pages are faded and worn so they are harder to read."

"How old are those books?" Doc asked, rubbing my thigh under the table in a platonic, calm-the-hell-down way.

"I'd say they were probably bound sometime during the medieval period. Many at the beginning are written on linen using quill and ink."

"No shit?" Reid said, leaning back in his chair.

Cornelius inspected the books with his head tipped to the side. "I might have a way of helping you translate and copy these stories to a more modern medium if you're interested."

I looked from Doc to Aunt Zoe, my heart still pounding hard. "I'm not sure I want to know what's on those pages."

"We went through this before, Violet Lynn," she whispered, not seeming very drunk for being a couple of whiskey slushes to the wind. "Hiding your head in the sand won't change the future."

"Maybe not," I whispered back. "But it might make the present less daunting to face every morning."

"Can I unplug my ears now?" Layne yelled.

I nodded at Doc, who reached over and tapped on Layne's hand. "Your mom's done cussing. For now, anyway."

Layne opened his eyes, his hazel gaze locking onto me. "Are you mad?"

"Yes."

That was the nitty-gritty truth under all of my ruffled feathers. Why did I have to be saddled with this Executioner crap? Why couldn't I be like everyone else and spend my nights worrying about paying bills and keeping the bullies away from my kids?

I was also scared shitless, but there was no way I could tell either of my kids that. I was their barometer when it came to incoming shitstorms. I had to keep my needle stuck on "Fair" at all times in the face of their fears, no matter how much my palms sweated and my knees shook.

"Are you mad at me or Aunt Zoe?" Layne asked.

"Neither of you. I just realized something when Aunt Zoe showed us these books that reminded me of a problem I need to deal with at work." There. That was also true, only it was cloaked in vagueness.

"Do you feel better now that you cussed about it?"

I shrugged. "Not really, but it was worth a try."

He turned back to Aunt Zoe. "How many more battles are in those books?"

She rested her hand on the stack. "These babies are chock full of many, many gladiator battles."

More nightmares, in other words.

Layne's grin stretched from ear to ear, his smile looking like the popcorn garland he'd been munching on earlier. "Cool!"

Not cool, I thought. Soooo not cool.

I scowled at the books with their leather binding and yellowed, rough-edged pages, imagining the grisly tales within them. Why couldn't we have come from simple German peasant stock and be known throughout the land for our thick thighs and vigorous loins?

Layne leaned over the table, practically salivating. "Are there pictures of the weapons?"

"There are a few drawings. Mostly these books are full of written descriptions of the enemies that the gladiators were dealing with in and around the Black Forest."

"Several centuries' worth of enemies," Doc said.

He was also frowning at the books. I was glad to see I wasn't alone in understanding the ramifications of three books' worth of bludgeoning and death.

"Centuries, Zo? Seriously?" Reid confirmed, sounding as flabbergasted as I felt.

"Yes, Martin. And before you ask, they weren't called the Dark Ages because the wind kept blowing out the candles."

Reid's gaze narrowed. "I'm going to enjoy teaching your smart mouth new tricks the next time we're alone."

She crossed her arms. "Come near me with those lips, and I'll bop you in the bazoo."

"Why so many battles?" Cornelius asked.

"Because Zo keeps fighting her feelings and chasing me away with her dang shotgun," Reid answered, almost grinning.

Aunt Zoe glared at her old flame, ruining her outraged act by hiccupping. "He was talking about the books."

"Yeah, but I wasn't."

She snorted and focused on Cornelius. "According to what my grandmother told me, the overall story in those books is about a territorial dispute going on under the surface during which various conflicts arose."

Under the surface? That struck a familiar chord.

I looked around the table. "Does anyone know how long mining has been happening in the Black Forest region of Germany?"

"Iron ore was being mined in the northern area since the fifth century BC, if I remember right," Doc said. His love of thick history books was paying off for me.

"I've read since Roman occupation times, certainly," Cornelius added.

Hmmm. I let that information set for a moment in my noggin. "How old are the land formations in and around the Black Forest?"

Doc's brow furrowed. "I read something about the South German Scarplands under the Black Forest forming in the Mesozoic era."

"Super. Could you translate that into my language?"

He smiled. "Between 65 to almost 250 million years ago."

"And how old are the Black Hills?"

"Old," he answered.

"Older than the Black Forest formation?"

"Almost two billion years older."

Double hmm. I spun the pencil I was using for the game in circles on the table.

"What's with all of these questions?" Aunt Zoe asked.

"Don't you find it interesting how similar the Black Forest and the Black Hills are?" I looked up. "I wonder how they compare in size."

"The Black Forest is a little narrower," Doc said. "But the lengths are similar."

Reid was right. My ancestors had moved from one hotspot to another. That couldn't be a mere coincidence, could it? Did it have something to do with mining deep into the earth? Was there another territorial dispute growing?

Those three books filled with pages of life and death

made me wonder if history was about to repeat itself in a new, yet similar location. Hell, all of the players were certainly lining up, including me and my twins.

"Whose turn is it?" Layne asked.

"I believe it's still Doc's turn." Aunt Zoe reached for her nearly empty glass of whiskey slush. "He was supposed to make a guess."

Doc looked at his cards and then the board. "How about Amityville Amy using the parascope while stuck in the haunted police station jail with Violet?"

Reid laughed. "That sounds typical of Coop's overly anal interrogation techniques, huh, Sparky?"

I nodded. "I have nothing to show you, Doc."

"I beg to differ," he said, making Aunt Zoe giggle.

As the task of proving Doc's guess wrong moved on to Aunt Zoe, I glanced his way. Doc was caught up in this Executioner mess, too. Our worlds hadn't collided by chance, not with the way he was able to help me navigate through the dark and open doors I couldn't see. We were part of something much bigger here.

I was beginning to suspect the same idea went for Cornelius, who was flipping through the more recent family history book again. Months ago, he'd walked into Calamity Jane Realty asking for me in particular to help him buy a haunted hotel. A short time after that, he and I had sat next to Wild Bill's grave while he taught me how to use a sixth sense I hadn't known was within me. That couldn't have been a coincidence either.

Who else was being sucked into this maelstrom? Natalie? Harvey? Cooper? Reid? My co-workers? Prudence the ghost? Rosy the—

Prudence!

I flinched as a bolt of realization struck me.

Of course.

"Mom?" Layne waved his hand in front of my face.

"Are you in there?"

"What? Is it my turn?"

Doc was watching me with one raised eyebrow. "You need more to drink?"

I shook my head. Not yet.

A toss of the dice later, I moved my token into the haunted hospital. My guess starring Winchester Wendy and the Mel meter didn't make it past Cornelius.

As play continued around me, I sat back in my chair and thought about that uppity Executioner ghost in Lead and some of Prudence's cryptic messages.

What had she said that time in the attic when she'd been using Doc as her ventriloquist doll? Something about it being too late?

Too many have been freed.

Maybe it was the tequila talking, but I could swear I heard her melodic, mid-Atlantic Eastern accent as if she were sitting next to me here at the table.

Too many what, Prudence? What else had she said?

Our enemy. They are numerous in the Hills.

Enemies like the bone cruncher? The chimera? The *lidérc*? More of the *others*? Dominick Masterson and his ilk?

You will not succeed on your own. Especially considering what they have already unleashed.

Caly unleashed the *lidérc*, but Prudence had shared this message prior to Caly's part in that mess.

I was the last of my line. That is why I remained. I was waiting for you … You need me.

Three books' worth of Dark Ages battles. How many battles had there been here in Deadwood in Prudence's time? How many more would there be in mine? In Addy's?

You are notorious, Violet. A Scharfrichter *from the Black Forest region. A very small world it is among our kind.*

I frowned at the stack of books. A small world indeed.

Your line has always been lacking finesse. Brutal even.

She was spot-on there. We were like juggernauts, rushing in swinging whatever mace, battle-ax, or tire iron we could take up in the heat of the moment.

They will end your line.

That's where she was wrong. I couldn't let them. We had pages and pages filled with our blood and sacrifice over the centuries.

You have wasted precious time, Scharfrichter.

Yeah, well, some of us took a little longer to come around to a killing way of thinking. I'd needed to get a few things straight in my mind first.

Your job is to protect. Not question.

She was wrong. My job was to protect *and* question. And if Prudence knew something about what was coming, she needed to give me less cryptic answers, damn it.

You smell of death.

I rolled my eyes. Okay, that was just plain rude on her part. Unfortunately, she wasn't the only non-human who had told me that. Had she smelled of death, too, when she was alive?

"Aunt Zoe?" Layne's voice pulled me out of my inward spiral. "Maybe you should write some stories about a gladiator from the Black Hills."

Out of the mouths of babes.

Aunt Zoe smirked at me. "Maybe I will, Layne. Maybe you and I could write a few together someday."

Was she priming him for the family trade? I thought a *magistra* had to be female. Then again, Ayla had mated with a Summoner and changed the cycle of having twin girls that had gone on for who knows how long, so maybe it was time for a …

Summoner.

Oh, shit!

"Layne," I said, as Reid picked up the dice. "Can you go upstairs and grab my black sweater, please?"

"But it's almost my turn."

"We'll wait for you," Doc said, eyeing me suspiciously.

Grumbling about a lack of child labor laws in this house, Layne stomped out of the room.

I didn't waste time. "Aunt Zoe," I whispered. "Does Layne have summoning abilities?"

"I don't know yet."

"You haven't seen any signs of him drawing *others* to him yet?"

She shook her head. "But I've tried to shield him since birth."

"Shield him how?" Doc asked.

"With charms carrying symbols that might mask his beacon, for lack of a better word at the moment."

She had always been giving me necklaces and trinkets for the kids to carry with them at all times. "Good luck charms, my ass. You've been taking precautions all of this time."

"Like Charan's sorceress mother," Cornelius said. "Very sly of you."

"Violet, your great-grandmother taught me well on the subject of protection. However, I worry that these concealments will only shield Layne for so long. If he truly is a Summoner, his strength will grow with age."

"But there may be some time yet before that happens?" Doc asked her. "Time to prepare him for what is to come?"

"Maybe. Or not. Violet's strengths are increasing tenfold. That might mean his are as well."

Reid leaned his elbows on the table. "Prepare how? Like with weapons?"

"You know, Violet," Cornelius said, rising with his empty plate and taking it to the sink. "I'm beginning to believe your son's preoccupation with weapons is determined more by genetics than a mere fascination. Are we certain his blood runs red?"

I wasn't certain of anything at this moment.

"Fuck." I scrubbed my hands down my cheeks. "This means he's even more of a target."

"Possibly," Aunt Zoe said. "However, he's not the only one we should be watching for signs of *Der Beschwörer*."

It took me a second to figure out that she'd used the old German word for Summoner. "He's not?"

"No, dear. You're forgetting another who stands in line in front of Layne."

I searched her blue eyes. "You mean my da—" Oh no! I covered my mouth. "Quint," I whispered through my fingers.

"Yes. Your father and I have been watching your brother as well over the years, waiting for signs of his transformation."

"Like what signs?" I thought about how healthy and strong Quint had looked over the Christmas holiday, as if he'd been working out more. "Physical changes?"

She nodded. "And nightmares, for starters. Changes similar to those you experienced when you were struggling to break free of your cocoon."

Cocoon? I might have used a coffin-related metaphor instead for this Executioner gig.

"Have you noticed anything different with Quint?" I asked.

"Not yet."

Whew! So maybe we had time before shit really started hitting the fan. Or maybe this Summoner business would skip over Quint entirely and slam head-on into Layne.

Aunt Zoe drew invisible doodles on the table. "If Quint does fall in line as the next Summoner, we might have a problem on our hands."

Besides the hair-raising fact that an Executioner *and* a Summoner had been awakened, for lack of a better word, to deal with whatever was coming our way?

"What's that?" I asked.

"A Summoner can set into motion widespread destruction and death."

"You mean like the *lidérc* and the bone cruncher and all of the *other* assholes I'm dealing with here in Deadwood?" Not including Detective Hawke, Doc's ex-girlfriend, and Rex the kids' sperm donor, of course. They were just regular assholes.

"Yes, and then some." Aunt Zoe looked at me, her worried expression making my heart thud in my ears again. "Without an Executioner nearby to kill whatever is drawn to Quint, he's a sitting duck. Although, as much as he travels, he might stay ahead of his enemies. Safely out of reach."

Or not.

I thought of the *lidérc* and how quickly it had shifted from one perceived loved one to another when it was trying to lure me into its parasitic embrace. Fortunately for me, it had gotten its wires screwed up and I'd seen through its deception. Would my brother be easier to fool?

"When is Quint leaving for Mexico?"

The lines on her face doubled. "Soon. Very soon."

Chapter Ten

New Year's Day
Deadwood, South Dakota

An hour later, midnight had come and gone, dragging off last year's messes behind it. I leaned against the kitchen counter, enjoying a moment alone with a tall, sexy medium. A mellow tequila buzz still filled my head, smoothing the bumpy ride into the new year.

Reid had won the last round of the game with a bawdy guess starring Winchester Wendy dancing around the fire pole in the haunted fire station wearing only a gauzy veil with the audio recorder blasting out Deep Purple's "Smoke on the Water." After Aunt Zoe had stopped laughing, she'd informed him that it was a handheld audio recorder, not some old-school boombox, and that Deep Purple's "Knocking at Your Back Door" would be better for pole dancing. Reid hadn't argued with her for once. Instead, he'd just smiled and stared at her like she was the one dancing around a pole in a veil.

After we'd packed away the game, Layne had conked out on the couch between Aunt Zoe and Reid while they watched the New Year's celebrations in different time zones on the television. I wondered if she'd go up to bed soon and if Reid would try to join her. Probably not. The risk of a backside full of birdshot was still too high.

Cornelius was currently sleeping in the recliner that Harvey usually occupied while he was here. Earlier, while he was still in the kitchen with me, I'd asked him if the number six was considered a magic number.

His reply had made my cheeks warm. "Six is the number of love."

Doc paused in the midst of wiping off the table. "I think I'll make that my new lucky number."

"What do you mean, it's the number of love?"

"Six symbolizes beauty and harmony. It's also prevalent throughout nature in the form of hexagons, such as with the honeycomb and tortoiseshells. Why do you have a newfound number obsession?"

"I don't have an obsession." I finished drying the last plate and handed it to Cornelius, who was helping me with the dishes. "Six kept coming up tonight for some reason."

"Of course it did. You were sitting safely in your aunt's kitchen surrounded by loved ones. The number six pertains to domestic life and the qualities needed for harmony, health, and happiness. It often symbolizes service to others, which is in essence your new role per your genetic line. I'm surprised you didn't recognize your relationship to the number six sooner, Aries."

"Yeah, well, I left my numerology glasses at work next to my astrology book." Besides, I sucked at relationships for most of my life. Doc was a happy anomaly. "So there's nothing bad about the number six showing up so much tonight?"

"Well, if memory serves, an imbalance of this number can lead to sacrificial tendencies. But that's a rare occurrence, so don't lose any sleep over it." He yawned, closing the cupboard door. "Although, you being an Aries, I don't expect that you enjoy much sleep."

"What do you mean?" My nightmares had been virtually non-existent since Doc joined me in my bed. "Do Aries tend to have sleep issues?"

"No." He watched Doc straighten the kitchen chairs. "Aries personalities are aggressive and impulsive, true warriors through and through."

"What does that have to do with sleeping?"

"Their sex lives are intense, and their need for coitus is insatiable."

Doc let out a shout of laughter.

"Years ago," Cornelius continued as if I wasn't standing before him sizzling clear to my toes with embarrassment, "I had sex repeatedly with an Aries who worked in the fairy booth at a traveling Renaissance fair. Her passions scared the hell out of me. I'd never experienced such vigorous animalistic lovemaking. I still have several bite scars from her." He lifted his shirt, showing a very pale chest.

A squawk escaped from my throat. I caught his hand, dragging his shirt back down. "No more sex talk tonight," I said and bulldozed him through the dining room, pushing him down into the recliner. "Stay."

"Everything okay?" Aunt Zoe asked.

"Aries are very passionate," Cornelius explained, tugging on the recliner lever.

I left the room before I melted in humiliation.

Doc's smile awaited me when I returned to the kitchen. "This Aries business explains a lot about you, Boots. I just hope I have the stamina to keep up with you. Maybe we should keep a first-aid kit on the nightstand."

I pointed at him. "You were no help."

Now, ten minutes later, Doc was still smiling as he leaned back against the counter next to me. "So what's the plan, Killer?"

"I'd like to try not to die."

"Not dying is always good," he agreed, taking my hand in his.

"And not have any of those whom I love die."

"I'm all for that."

"But yet kill anything that threatens my family and friends."

He linked his fingers through mine. "So, we're choosy about deaths. Got it."

"Exactly. And I have to wait for Natalie to return before I start hunting the *lidérc*."

"So that we can sacrifice her?" he joked.

I smiled. "I doubt Cooper would allow that to happen these days." Speaking of Cooper's crush on Natalie ... "I wonder how things are going in Arizona with those two."

"You haven't talked to Natalie recently?"

"No, she's been quiet. I almost texted her earlier, but I believe Cooper was dead serious when he told you to tell me he'd arrest me if I interfered with his pursuit."

"He certainly wasn't smiling when he made the threat."

"But I'm curious as hell if Natalie will go off her sabbatical for him." She'd given up men for a year back in July. Months into it, Cooper had started circling her lifeboat.

I tried to picture what it would be like for the bristly detective to woo a woman, but my mind kept having him slap handcuffs on her and not in a sexy way. His idea of foreplay was probably reading Natalie her Miranda rights.

"So why do you have to wait for Natalie to return?"

"Because she told me that if I do anything dangerous without her here to help, she'll dye my eyebrows black while I sleep."

He looked at my eyebrows. "With your curly hair, you'd be a mixture of Groucho and Harpo Marx."

I wiggled my eyebrows, Groucho Marx style, and pretended to talk around a cigar, quoting one of his lines I remembered, "Why, I'd horse-whip you if I had a horse."

Doc joined my cigar pretending. "Who are you going to believe, me or your own eyes?" he said, shooting another

Marx line back at me.

When we stopped snickering, I sighed. "These days, I'd probably believe you. I've been seeing some shit that boggles my mind lately."

"You and me both." He kissed the back of my hand.

"Plus, it's probably wise to wait for Cooper in case whatever happens gets me into trouble with the law."

"You mean *more* trouble."

"That, too. Detective Hawke is itching to take me to jail and drop the key down the nearest mine shaft."

"Don't forget about your bodyguard," Doc said. "He'd be a sad sack if he missed out on more shotgun fun."

"I wonder if Harvey's keeping out of trouble down in Arizona."

Doc grinned. "Not if he has a say in it."

I leaned my head against his shoulder. "We need to talk to Prudence again."

"Yeah." He sounded as excited about it as I felt.

"But I don't want you to be her microphone."

"Because I see you naked on a regular basis?"

"No, because I see *you* naked, and if I hear Prudence's voice coming out of your mouth again, I may need to join a nunnery and spend the rest of my life spinning in a mountain valley full of wildflowers."

"You do realize, Violet, that not all nunneries are located in the Austrian alps, right?"

"You get the idea."

"Who do you have in mind to help you converse with Prudence?"

"She said before that Zelda is a wide-open channel for her, so we'll start with her. But I think I should bring Cornelius along next time."

"Why him?"

"I don't know, but it seems like when he does his rhythmic humming during séances, I'm able to channel better and reach farther."

"I want to be there with you."

"But—"

"No buts, Killer. Somehow or other, there has to be a way for me to be there with you when you talk to her. We'll figure this out, but not tonight. We have other things to discuss."

"Like what?"

"For one thing, how you're going to catch a *lidérc*."

"Right, that small matter. What else?"

"Are you going to tell your brother about the whole Summoner business?"

"Not yet. It's not something you blurt out over the phone, and I'm not sure when he'll be back in town again. Besides, if he's not dealing with any freaky shit, why open that door?"

"He needs to know about you."

"Sure. Eventually." I looked around my aunt's lemony yellow kitchen. "Standing here right now with you, it seems like one big nightmare. That the stories in those books are merely what Layne thinks they are—random tales about gladiator women."

"Rather than tomes full of family traditions."

I scoffed. "More like fatal traditions. Honestly, Doc, I don't know why you'd want to come near me after hearing some of those stories."

"You're forgetting that I'd already read them before tonight." He tugged me into his arms, his gaze tender when he tucked a strand of hair behind my ear. "Finally, my life is starting to make sense. Knowing what you are and your purpose here might be initially daunting. Trust me, I understand that. But I have faith in you … in *us*."

I spread my fingers over his chest, soaking up his warmth and stability. "Do you think Ayla ever felt uncertain? Did she question who she was and what she needed to do?"

"Being that she was part human, I would imagine she went through some of the same self-doubts most of us do. But like you will do, she did what had to be done." He untied my sweater belt and reached inside, palming my hips. "If she was anything near as charming and beautiful as you, poor Charan didn't have a chance in hell of not falling head over heels in love with her."

"Ah, now you're just trying to butter me up, hoping I'll let you share my bed tonight."

"I'm that obvious, huh?"

I pressed against him, breathing in the smell of his woodsy cologne as well as something sweet. Or maybe that was me. "Crystal clear, Candy Cane."

"It's the first day of a new year," he said, pulling me even closer, giving me an up-close-and-personal idea of his terrain. "We should start it out right."

I batted my lashes at him. "You mean by slamming shots of tequila?"

"For starters, yes."

I reached around him and grabbed the salt shaker and a slice of lemon. I licked the back of my hand and poured some salt on it, holding it out to him. "Here, lick the salt."

His eyes creased in the corners. "Harvey would tell you that was supposed to be my line."

"Just lick but don't swallow."

Chuckling under his breath, he obeyed.

I held the lemon slice in front of his face. "Now stick this in your mouth and suck."

His laughter rumbled, low and deep. "Again, my line."

I slapped his shoulder. "Quit channeling that dirty old buzzard and open your mouth."

"Okay, but I thought the lemon came after the tequila."

"We're mixing it up." I set the lemon wedge between his lips. "Now suck."

While he followed my directions, I licked salt off of the back of my hand and sucked on another lemon wedge. Then I tipped back the bottle and took a long draw, washing it all down together.

Doc took the bottle from me and did the same, grimacing slightly as it went down. "Damn, that first one always feels like it goes down sideways on fire."

I set the bottle down. "Come on, tough guy. Don't let a little girl like me outdrink you. How about another one?"

"I'd rather have a shot of this."

He kissed me, tasting like lemon and tequila, delivering a fiery punch on his own.

I looped my arms around his neck, molding my body against his. "Let's go to bed," I whispered when I came up for air, rising up on my toes for a second shot of Doc.

"I hate to interrupt," Aunt Zoe said from behind me. "But your son is summoning."

I stiffened, turning toward her with a frown. "What?"

"He's summoning Doc."

"Doc?" The man in question met my raised eyebrows with a pair of his own.

"Yep." She reached under the sink and pulled out a big yellow bowl.

"Oh, no," I said. "Not the puke bowl."

"When I took Layne up to bed, we detoured into the bathroom and things took a turn for the worse while he brushed his teeth."

"Crud," I muttered. "I shouldn't have let him have so much root beer." And lemon bars, and cookies, and whatever else he ate while I was dealing with our family history. "Do I need to clean up the bathroom?"

"I took care of that, but he wants Doc to come up and tell him some ghost stories until he falls asleep again."

I looked up at Doc. "If you don't want to … I mean, I don't want you to feel like you're stuck going up there with him, because dealing with a sick kid is … I can go and tell him that you …" The rise of one of his eyebrows made me stop stepping all over my tongue. "What?"

"If you're about done finding excuses that I don't need, I have a Summoner waiting for me to keep him company."

I wrinkled my nose at him. "Holler for me if he starts throwing up again."

"Maybe, baby," he said, dropping a kiss on my forehead. He took the puke bowl from Aunt Zoe on his way out of the kitchen.

Aunt Zoe turned to me after he left. "Layne wanted Doc," she said for my ears only.

"So you said." I pushed the cork into the mostly empty bottle of wine. The passionate and aggressive Aries in me wanted Doc, too, but a sick kid trumped hot, animalistic sex every time, dang it.

"That's a good thing, don't you think?" She sat on the edge of the table, watching me.

"Very good. Keep your fingers crossed he doesn't throw up on Doc and chase him away."

"I think Doc can handle a little vomit."

"Where's Reid sleeping tonight?" I asked, closing up the whiskey bottle.

"Not in my bed."

"That's not very hospitable of you."

"Ha! You invited him, let him sleep in your bed with you and Doc."

"I think he'd much rather warm your sheets. Is Cornelius taking Addy's bed?"

Aunt Zoe nodded. "Reid can sleep on the couch."

"That's a back breaker. I really need to get you a new couch."

She crossed her arms. "If I wanted a new couch, I'd buy one."

I set the wine and whiskey bottles on top of the

refrigerator. "Have you ever wondered what would've happened if you'd married Reid the first time around."

"First of all, that makes it sound like there will be a second time around, and that is a delusion."

"You know what I mean."

She looked toward the living room, her upper lip lined. "We'd have been married for better or worse, I guess."

"What about kids?"

She shook her head without even thinking about it.

"I thought you liked kids."

"I love children, but I've known since I was a little girl that I'd never have any of my own."

"How?" Was there some physical ailment interfering with her ability to have kids that she hadn't told me about?

"When I was training under your great-grandmother, she told me that not once in all of the times she consulted the rune stones did my future have children in it. I was barren, and I needed to be okay with that."

"But rune stones only show possible paths to your future. Their results are not fixed."

"Some things were not meant to be, Violet. Me having children was one of those." At my sad face, she said, "It's okay. I've been able to enjoy more time with you and your brother because I had no kids of my own. Sometimes being an aunt is as wonderful as being a parent—only without all the yelling," she finished with a grin.

I moaned about my yelling hellions. I wouldn't know about that—not yet, anyway. But maybe Quint would be a father someday and I'd get to see if that was true for myself. If we both lived long enough, that was. Lord help us all if Susan decided to spawn a child.

Speaking of parenting, "I hope Addy didn't follow in her brother's shoes and eat too much junk food tonight."

"I'm sure Jeff Wymonds can handle a sick kid after dealing with his own for years." She looked me up and down. "So, what are you going to do next?"

"Do you want a list of my New Year's resolutions?"

"You know what I mean, child."

"Getting into shape is NOT on the list this year. I'm finished with exercising unless it involves an ice cream truck or sex."

"Violet Lynn."

Okay, okay. "Well, for starters, I'm going to catch a *lidérc* for Dominick Masterson. Just call me Violet Parker, *Scharfrichter* for Hire." This one time, anyway. After this deal was settled, I was closing up shop and working only for myself.

"I still don't love this idea."

"I have to get Dominick off your back."

"Fine." Aunt Zoe linked her fingers together. "But you'll be taking me along to help."

While I was open to help from others now, I worried about her getting too close to Dominick. "This isn't your fight."

"Yes, it is. Besides, there's something I didn't tell you earlier in front of Doc and the others." The troubled expression on her face reminded me of my great-grandmother when I'd enter the room during her rune stones fun and games—a mixture of wariness and unease. "It's something Grandmother told me a few days before she died that the runes showed her repeatedly about *you*."

Not this great-grandmother crapola again. "If it's that I carry hidden dangers in my pocket, I already have that shit burned into my brain, thank you very much."

"It's not—" she started but then stopped. "Well, yes, she did say that about you many times as well, but this was something different."

Marvelous. Why couldn't my great-grandmother have been one of those sweet old ladies who liked to give her great-grandkids hard mint candies and stale cookies? Hell,

I'd have taken crusty black licorice in place of her creepy looks and skin-crawling predictions about my future.

"She said—"

"Wait," I told Aunt Zoe. I grabbed the bottle of tequila off the counter, not messing with the salt or lemon to smooth the way down, and took a swig. Coughing into my arm, I waved her to continue. "I'm all ears."

"And tequila."

"Don't worry, I'm sober enough to tie my shoes still."

"You're wearing slippers."

"Close enough. Tell me what my wonderfully sweet and cuddly great-grandma said about me on her death bed."

"Not quite her death bed."

"Aunt Zoe." I stuck my hands on my hips.

She smiled, but it was grim. "Okay." She chewed on her lower lip, eyeing me as if I might make a run for it at any moment.

Running was certainly a possibility these days.

"She said that when the time came for you to fulfill your role in the family line, you would fail."

"Sheesh! She didn't even let me get out of the gate before shooting me down."

"Unless," Aunt Zoe continued, holding up her finger, "there were more than one of you to take up the fight."

My eyes narrowed. "You're just saying that so I'll drag you along with me on the hunt."

"No, Violet. You don't understand." She stood and came closer, standing in front of me while staring into my eyes. "She didn't mean you and me—or you and your friends. She meant more than one Executioner."

My breath caught. "But Addy's too young."

"I know."

"So who else could there b…"

You need me, Prudence had said.

"Son of an uppity bitch." I slapped my forehead.

"There'll be no living with Prudence once I tell her she was right, that I do need her."

"True," Aunt Zoe said, pulling me into a hug. "But maybe if you play your cards right with Prudence, there'll be no dying either."

The End ... for now

About the Author

Ann Charles is a USA Today bestselling author who writes award-winning mysteries that are splashed with humor, romance, paranormal, and whatever else she feels like throwing into the mix. When she is not dabbling in fiction, arm-wrestling with her children, attempting to seduce her husband, or arguing with her sassy cats, she is daydreaming of lounging poolside at a fancy resort with a blended margarita in one hand and a great book in the other.

Facebook (Personal Page):
http://www.facebook.com/ann.charles.author

Facebook (Author Page):
http://www.facebook.com/pages/Ann-Charles/37302789804?ref=share

Twitter (as Ann W. Charles):
http://twitter.com/AnnWCharles

Ann Charles Website:
http://www.anncharles.com

More Books by Ann

Books in the Deadwood Mystery Series

WINNER of the 2010 Daphne du Maurier Award for Excellence in Mystery/Suspense

WINNER of the 2011 Romance Writers of America® Golden Heart Award for Best Novel with Strong Romantic Elements

Welcome to Deadwood—the Ann Charles version. The world I have created is a blend of present day and past, of fiction and non-fiction. What's real and what isn't is for you to determine as the series develops, the characters evolve, and I write the stories line by line. I will tell you one thing about the series—it's going to run on for quite a while, and Violet Parker will have to hang on and persevere through the crazy adventures I have planned for her. Poor, poor Violet. It's a good thing she has a lot of gumption to keep her going!